MARSHMALLOWS AND MEMORIES

THE PERIDALE CAFE SERIES - BOOK 25

AGATHA FROST

About This Book

Released: *November 8th 2022*
Words: *58,000*
Series: *Book 25 - Peridale Cozy Café Mystery Series*
Standalone: *Yes*
Cliff-hanger: *No*

After a busy summer apart, the cold autumn nights and the wedding of Johnny and Leah brings Julia and her old school friends back together. And with hardly any time to go, Julia is struggling to adapt her home baking skills to the autumnal spectacular Leah has dreamt up for her big day's wedding cake. Flavor is one thing Julia can nail, but the pictures last a lifetime.

The wedding cake experiments soon get put on the backburner when the body of one of their former teachers, Felicity Campbell, is found buried in a time capsule at the school. Along with her private investigator husband, Barker, her daughter, Jessie, and her best friend and fellow bridesmaid - and teacher - Roxy, Julia finds herself in the middle of a complicated unsolved missing person's case from 30 years ago.

What happened in 1989 to result in Felicity's burial in a time capsule, and why did everyone think she was living peacefully in Scotland? With those she left behind still in the village, and Barker officially on the case, they have access to all of the suspects, but not everybody is telling the truth about their last meeting with Miss Campbell. With the wedding creeping closer, Julia must juggle the cake and case, but can she close the lid on the mystery before the big day?

WANT TO BE KEPT UP TO DATE WITH AGATHA FROST RELEASES? *SIGN UP THE FREE NEWSLETTER!*

www.AgathaFrost.com

You can also follow **Agatha Frost** across social media. Search 'Agatha Frost' on:

Facebook
Twitter
Goodreads
Instagram

ALSO BY AGATHA FROST

Other

MARSHMALLOWS AND MEMORIES

Peridale Café Book 25

By Agatha Frost

October 29th

1

*P*ink and white marshmallows hit Julia
South-Brown's top lip as she sipped from
a mug of steaming hot chocolate. The wind howled
outside, but Julia was protected by the warmth of her
café's kitchen. A frustrated sigh escaped her, though it
had nothing to do with the chilly start to November or
the café's latest addition to the menu. The maple and
cinnamon-infused drink – using real chocolate
instead of the powdered stuff – was delicious. All the
credit for the new hot-selling item went to her
daughter, Jessie.

Julia glanced at the beaded curtain to check on
Jessie. From her hunched shoulders as she leaned
across the counter, she was scrolling on her phone,
which was fine by Julia. The café always filled up on

Bonfire Night – November 5th – but the bitter wind had kept people in their homes so far. The vans carrying wood to the bonfire's usual location in the field behind St. Peter's Church was the most activity they'd seen all day.

Julia took another sip of the rich and creamy drink and returned her attention to the kitchen island. If the café had been as busy as she'd foretold that morning, she might not have spent so much of her day in the kitchen creating tests for Leah and Johnny's wedding cake. She stemmed another sigh with a purse of her lips, but her sentiment toward her efforts was the same.

She didn't like it.

She didn't like it at all.

The small sample layer of pumpkin spice fruit cake underneath the white marzipan and her decoration was delicious. Rich and gooey with the lingering warmth that the season commanded, she'd nailed the recipe earlier in the week. But the decoration? Given how many hours she'd spent that afternoon, she'd need to clone herself to perfect the techniques required to create Leah's dream before the cake cutting.

The wedding was in less than three weeks.

Julia checked the reference pictures Leah had emailed to her that weekend. Though she was a wedding planner in her professional life, it had taken Leah a painfully long time to settle on a colour scheme and a theme for the wedding. With every new direction came a new vision for the cake. After changing the scheme from rich purple to warm autumnal colours, Leah had promised this was the last change. Julia had been glad to swap the shiny satin purple dress that had made her look like a Cadbury's Dairy Milk wrapper for the much nicer dress of rust-coloured chiffon. Still, the plan for the purple cake had been less complicated. Julia could have created the cascade of flowers Leah had wanted with a piping bag and some patience.

Julia zoomed in on the picture, and her stomach flipped. The cascade remained, but the flowers had been replaced with crisp autumn leaves. A small change that Julia had been assured should be 'straight-forward' when Leah had verbally described her vision over coffee on Saturday. The pictures Leah emailed on Monday had worried Julia in a way a cake project hadn't in a while.

Leah didn't want straight-forward.

She wanted spectacular.

"It's as dead as a doornail in here," Jessie said as she poked her head through the beads. "How's the cake coming along?"

"See for yourself."

Jessie joined Julia in looking at the flat-looking leaves she'd stuck to the side of the sample layer. The silence said it all.

"They're not bad."

"They're not good, either." Julia bit her lip and zoomed in on the leaves in the reference picture. "Whoever created this seems to be an expert in photorealism. Those leaves look like they were plucked from the village green. I'm out of my depth."

"They do look rather crispy. You did a great job on that globe cake for my 'Welcome Home' party, and I saw pictures of that nail varnish bottle you made for Katie's Salon."

"They pushed me to the edge of what I'm capable of, and they still looked cartoonish. Leah wants a David Attenborough documentary filmed in sparkling clear 8K resolution." Julia zoomed out and flicked to the following reference picture showing the second cake. The bottom tier had been decorated to look exactly like a slice of a tree trunk. "She wants it combined with this, and I'm as clueless about how to bring it to life as I am the leaves. It looks so real. I zoomed in for chainsaw marks when I first saw it. I blame *The Great British Bake Off* for making people think every baker can pull a showstopper out of their back pocket at a moment's notice."

Jessie laughed. "First of all, relax. Second, you're

the best baker in Peridale, and everyone knows it. I didn't call you Cake Lady when we first met for nothing."

"But you didn't call me Photorealistic Cake Decorating Lady." Julia joined Jessie in laughing. "My mum taught me how to bake, and funnily enough, that chapter is missing from her handwritten recipe book."

The bell above the café's front door announced a customer.

"I've got this one," Julia said. "I don't think I can take looking at my limp leaves for another second."

"They're not *that* bad," Jessie said with a wink. "And you've got *this* too. If anyone can pull this off, it's you, Cake Lady. You just have to be*leaf* in yourself."

Leaving Jessie to start washing up the small stack of mugs and plates that had built up over the slow day, Julia pushed through the beads into the café, where the scent of fresh paint still lingered. She thought the wind had moved the door until she saw the red hair of one of her oldest friends, Roxy Carter, bent over the small display case. Usually it only held small items such as cupcakes and brownies, but currently it was crammed with as many cakes as it could contain. The new revolving display cabinet still hadn't shown up.

"Latte?"

"I'm only passing through," Roxy said, her nose

close to the glass. "Help me out, mate. Which cake would you use if you were going to bribe someone?"

"Bribery? Anything I should be worried about?"

Roxy tapped at the last slice of the banoffee cake with a marshmallow fluff layer. "This one seems popular."

"Well, it depends on who you're trying to bribe."

"It's for a job interview."

Julia was surprised. "You're leaving the school?"

"The new job *is* at the school." Roxy straightened up with a frown on her brow. "Mr Harkup is finally retiring as headteacher, and I've thrown my hat into the ring."

"I want to say that's amazing news, but you don't seem pleased?"

"Because I don't stand a chance," Roxy said, her sigh anything but hopeful. "Hence the need for a bribe."

"Your two decades of teaching experience will work better than sugar." Julia transferred the slice to a cardboard box. "But you're right. This has been popular."

"I'm not even the most qualified for the job. I must have been crazy when I put my name forward. Maybe it's not too late to back out."

"When's the interview?"

"At five." Roxy glanced at the clock on the wall,

now half past four. "What was I thinking? I'm in way over my head. I should save myself the embarrassment and just pull out before this goes any further."

"What do you have to lose by going?"

"My dignity?"

"You lost that years ago, my friend." Julia raised a chuckle from Roxy, who'd been lacking her usual humour since she'd entered the café. "Look, I haven't been to a job interview in a long time, but from where I'm standing, you won't have lost anything even if you go and make a complete fool of yourself. This must be something you really want, or you wouldn't be so worried about it. At least give it a go."

Roxy huffed, looking at the clock.

"And I thought things would get less scary with age."

"We're forty-one. We're not dead yet."

"Try telling that to Leah. Has she told you about the hen party plans yet? Spa trip." Roxy rolled her eyes as she backed away from the counter. "Knowing Leah, it'll be the best spa in the Cotswolds. But what's wrong with a good ol' fashioned girls' night on the town? Are you going to be at the bonfire later?"

"Should be."

"As bridesmaids, I think we owe her an intervention before she regrets not blowing off steam one last time before she settles down for an eternity with Johnny Watson." Roxy pulled on the door. "Wish me luck."

"I take it that means you're going to the interview?"

"Might as well." Roxy shrugged, her hands going into her pockets as the wind whipped around her. "You're right. I don't have anything to lose." Roxy's eyes went around the café, and with a wave of her finger, she asked, "Have you redecorated?"

"Yes," Julia said with a wave. "Good luck."

The café door swung shut, and Roxy walked in the same direction as another van carrying more wood past the still village green. The last of the day's light was fading quickly, though it had been one of those gloomy days where the sun barely bothered to appear in the wash of pale grey above. With the bonfire starting in just over two hours and the cold wind still whipping around Peridale, Julia wondered if it was worth keeping the café open. Wanting to get Jessie's opinion, she pushed through the beaded curtains, where she was immediately distracted by her younger daughter, Olivia. From her perch in Barker's arms, Olivia reached out and plucked one of the leaves from the cake, which went straight to her mouth.

"Ah, ah, ah," Barker warned, placing it back in the

cluster. "That's Mummy's cake. Very abstract. What's it supposed to be?"

"Leaves."

Barker tilted his head as he passed Olivia over to Julia, though Olivia's attention was still on the cake. At least it had one fan.

"Uh-oh," Olivia remarked.

Maybe not.

"That one popped out today," Barker said, rubbing her plump cheek with the back of his finger. "Spilled her juice all over my case notes and hasn't been able to stop saying it, have you, Olivia?"

"Uh-oh."

"Ominous," Jessie said, glancing up from her phone. "That brings the grand total up to three words. Impressive. 'Mama', 'Dada', and 'uh-oh'. 'Jessie', when?"

Julia squeezed Olivia, always a tonic at the end of a workday. "Case notes? Anything interesting?"

"Just this stalking case," he said. "And by stalking, I mean the woman who thinks her husband is having an affair."

"Isn't that all of your clients?" Jessie asked.

"It's starting to feel like it. If tonight's the same as yesterday, I'm in for a night of taking pictures of him working alone in his office. To say I'd kill for something thrilling is an understatement."

"You and me both, Dad," Jessie said with a yawn.

"I'll try and make it back for the bonfire. I've been thinking about fire-toasted marshmallows all week."

Barker left through the back door, and Jessie returned to the café, leaving Julia to stare at her attempts at crispy leaves. She wasn't surprised Barker hadn't been able to figure out what they were. The distance she'd gained while talking to Roxy made Julia dislike her work even more. They looked like deflated starfish. Like Roxy, she felt out of her depth, but she asked herself the same question she'd asked her friend.

What's the worst that can happen?

If she didn't nail this, the cake would live on forever in the wedding pictures. Julia had no option. She wasn't going to back down from Leah's challenge, and there was no way she would tell her to find someone else. Not for Leah and Johnny's wedding. A wedding cake was the best gift she could give them, and she had offered.

There was only one thing for it.

If Leah wanted a photorealistic autumnal spectacular, that's what Julia would give her. She needed to look at it from a different angle than icing and food colouring.

"What's this cake box on the counter for?"

The different angle could wait until tomorrow.

She couldn't look at the leaves for another second.

"Roxy forgot her bribe," Julia called back, already grabbing her coat from the hook. "You okay to watch the café for ten minutes?"

Typical.

After waiting for the new display cabinet to arrive all week, of course the final piece of their renovation project came minutes after the door closed behind Julia and Olivia. Jessie directed the delivery men to put it next to the counter. After a slash of their pocketknife, they unwrapped the light layer of plastic around it, handed Jessie a phone to scribble her finger on, and went on their way.

Picking up Julia's abandoned maple and cinnamon hot chocolate, Jessie looked at the gigantic new case as the platforms revolved without a cake for the new lights to shine on. It could hold triple the amount, according to Julia. And so far, it wasn't making the humming noise of the old one, though Julia had always sworn she could never hear it. Something to do with young ears, apparently.

From the warm oak flooring that had replaced the tiles to the soft yellow walls above the new cream wood panelling, the café had undergone a total transformation in the six weeks since Jessie's homecoming. As shocked as she'd been to return to a café destroyed by festival rioters at the end of summer, the thugs had done them a favour. Even on a dreary November day, the café had never looked as fresh and modern. And Jessie had never been the biggest fan of the pink and blue cupcake wallpaper, though she'd kept that to herself. Julia had squealed with excitement when she'd found it during their last overhaul.

Jessie sipped the hot chocolate. She'd recreated the drink from memory based on one she'd loved in a cabin coffee shop in the Alps, where she'd learned she was a better snowboarder than skier. Those early days travelling with Alfie already felt so long ago. Not for the first time that day, she opened up her older brother's most recent message.

Alfie grinned up at her in a picture from New Zealand. On the other side of the world, it was a bright summer's day, and it looked like he was on the fruit-picking farm he'd told her he was working at during their last video call. It couldn't have been further from her current reality.

Jessie wondered what she was missing out on.

After nine months on the road, she'd grown too used to the ever-changing places and faces. Always a new local delicacy to taste, a new museum to wander around, a beauty spot to hunt down, with new sights, sounds, and smells waiting for them around every corner. And then onto a plane, a bus, or a boat to take them somewhere new to start again.

As homesick as she'd been at times, the nomadic nature of their lives had been strangely familiar to Jessie. It was something she was far too used to. She'd spent her childhood and teen years being uprooted and moved on, handed around like a game of pass the parcel where the prize was a foster child who didn't quite fit anywhere.

Peridale was the only place she'd ever stood still.

The pang passed, and she took another sip of her hot chocolate. Jessie was glad to be home, really. But as she stared at the new revolving display case, after all of her adventures, she couldn't help but wonder how hot chocolate and a new café gadget were the week's highlights.

The hot chocolate was delicious and the cabinet was snazzy, but her old Peridale life needed a dash more excitement.

2

*J*ulia clung tighter to the pram handle as she hurried across St. Peter's Primary School playground. The rubber wheels crunched over a carpet of crisp leaves as the wind swirled them around, revealing flashes of the painted-on hopscotch grids. They were in the same place as when she'd attended the school as a girl. She picked up her pace. She couldn't shake the eeriness washing over her. All of her memories of her childhood school were set against bright skies. Visiting after dark felt forbidden.

Pivoting away from the main entrance doors that led to the brightly lit reception area, Julia continued around the side of the school toward the sound of growling machinery. Diggers munched at the patch of grass outside Roxy's classroom, where the lights were on behind the closed blinds. The workmen operating the machines glanced at Julia as she pushed the pram along the narrow path covered in mud, but they carried on with their work as she continued trespassing.

Julia was glad to see Roxy behind her desk. Her eyes were clenched, and she seemed to be working through a breathing exercise. Not wanting to startle her friend, Julia tickled her nails on the glass. Roxy bolted upright in her chair, alarmed anyway.

"You left your bribe."

"As much as you didn't have to bring it," Roxy said, pulling Julia into a hug after letting her in, "I'm so glad to see a friendly face right now. I really don't think I can do this."

Roxy collapsed into the spinning chair behind her desk and scooped out the cake. She took a bite, and the taste of the banana and caramel sponge seemed to lift her spirits for a moment. Positioning the pram so Olivia could watch the diggers, Julia flipped one of the chairs from the table. She sat in the tiny chair, and her chin barely cleared the desk.

"I know it was for a bribe, but I don't think it'll make a difference," Roxy said, plucking the cake from the box. "I think I was hoping someone who knew me would try and snap me out of thinking I stood a chance."

"Well, you chose the wrong woman," Julia said with a smile, "because I have every faith in you, Roxy Carter. Always have, and always will. What's Violet think about all of this?"

"She's away for a family thing," Roxy said with a waft of her hand before going for a bite. Through the mouthful, she said, "I think I'd be less nervous if those diggers weren't making so much noise. I could barely get through my lessons today. Delicious, by the way."

"What are they building?"

"New bathrooms, and about fifteen years too late. Do you ever get the urge to dig up your life and start again?"

"Not recently."

"But you did once," Roxy said, continuing to talk through the chewing of another bite. "This time a decade ago, you were living in London, married to someone else. That woman would barely recognise you now."

"For the better."

"But you only know that now *because* you can look back. What's on your dartboard?"

"Are you expecting me to tell you I have an arch nemesis?"

"Not quite." Roxy laughed, finishing the cake. "You

only built a new life because you were aiming your dart at something. A vision of the future. Look at everything you have now."

Julia thought back to those difficult days post-separation and pre-divorce. The idea of opening a café had dragged her through the worst of it. The thought of adopting, re-marrying, or having a baby hadn't even crossed her mind.

"I think I know what you're feeling," Julia said, leaning her arms on the desk. "You feel aimless?"

"Aimless." Roxy investigated the empty cake box with a sigh. "I love teaching, I really do. As hard as it is, the kids make it worth it. I can't go a day without one of them making me laugh. That's what keeps me coming back. You know me, I've never been able to take anything too seriously. But, I don't know, I need a shake-up."

"Wanting change is normal."

"I don't just want *change*," Roxy said, staring off into the middle distance. "You know what I realised on my forty-first birthday? Firstly, I probably should have invested in getting some Botox about ten years ago." Roxy scrunched up her face. "But the thing that really hit me as I was blowing out my candles in the staffroom for the twentieth year in a row was that I didn't want the next twenty years to be the same as the last. Since Harkup announced he was finally throwing in the towel, I've been excited about coming to work. Excited in a way I haven't been since I finished my teacher training. I don't just want change. I *need* a challenge. I really thought *this* was it."

"You haven't even had your interview yet, Rox. Why are you so sure you don't stand a chance?"

"Because Mr Harkup's daughter is the obvious shoo-in for the job," she whispered, glancing to the corridor. "Molly Harkup. She teaches Year Six. It's like they crafted the perfect teacher in a lab and gifted her to the world. She's in the assembly hall right now painting the sets for the autumn production she's directing, and I'd bet she was first in this morning for breakfast club. I can't even deny that she's perfect for the job, but I just wanted to see what would happen if I—"

The phone gave two short rings, cutting Roxy off.

"Is that your cue?"

Roxy nodded with a gulp.

"I think it's time for you to see what will happen."

"Will you wait for me?" Roxy stood up and tugged down the creases in her blazer. "I think I'll need a hug when it's all over. I've missed your hugs. I feel like I've barely seen you lately. I'm so glad this wedding has brought us back together."

"Me too." Julia gave her a final squeeze. "I'll be right here."

Alone, Julia took in the classroom in which she'd once been a student. An electronic whiteboard had replaced the one of chalk, and the tables and chairs had been refreshed, though the room still felt the same, even from her taller viewpoint. She could almost see herself there with Roxy, Johnny, and Leah, as though no time had passed. Olivia babbled, reminding her how much time *had* passed.

"Won't be long until you're a student here," she said, joining Olivia at the door. "What's going on out there?"

Olivia answered with a gurgle as Julia peered through the window. The diggers had stopped operating, and the two workmen stared into the hole they'd created. Under the bright lights projecting down on their worksite, their worried expressions were clear.

"What do we do?" one of them asked.

"Dunno," the other replied with a shrug. "Let's pull it out."

One jumped into the hole, while the other stayed on the edge. A long oblong appeared from the mud. It looked to be made of earth, too, but the shape was angular, and from their heaving grunts, it had a considerable weight to it. They dumped it on the grass, both scratching their heads. One of them gave it a kick. A hollow metallic thud echoed back. Some of the mud crumbled off, revealing dulled stainless steel.

"Let's get it inside. Headteacher can figure out what to do with it.

"We *are* already behind schedule."

Julia opened the door and dragged the pram out of the way. The two workmen carried in the object by its handles. They hurried through the classroom and into the corridor, leaving a dirt trail on the shiny floor. Julia closed the door, wrapped her hands around the pram, and followed. She was more than a little intrigued by what they'd found.

Avoiding the trail of mud with the pram wheels, Julia followed them to the entrance area between the reception and the main hall. The hall, the space where she'd eaten her lunches, sat on the cold tiles for assembly, and taken part in PE lessons seemed unchanged. However, she couldn't believe how much smaller it seemed compared to her childhood memories.

On the other side of the hall, a woman was up a stepladder, rolling red paint onto a large MDF board behind the stage. Judging by the giant playing cards that had already been painted onto one side, the school would soon see a production of *Alice in Wonderland*. Julia wondered if the painter was the Year Six teacher Roxy had told her about.

"What do we do with it?" one of the workmen whispered. "Shall we just ditch it here?"

"Why not? Not our problem."

"Yeah, not our problem."

The silver box went down into the middle of the corridor between the reception and the hall, and more mud fell off on contact with the pale blue tiles. The men dusted off their hands and left. Parking the pram by the wall, Julia approached the box.

What was it?

There were numbers etched on the stainless steel.

19...

She dusted off more of the mud.

1990

Why did Julia feel like she'd seen the box before?

"Excuse me," a voice filled with familiar teacher authority echoed around the hall. "Can I help you?"

Julia turned as the woman with the paint roller walked to her in a long flowing skirt made of multi-coloured layers and a knitted brown cardigan. When she got close enough, Julia saw 'Miss Harkup' on the ID badge around her neck. Given her greying edges, she seemed to be in her fifties.

"Hi," Julia said, retrieving the pram. "I know I shouldn't be here, but—"

"The children were let out of rehearsals an hour

ago," she said, squinting at Julia. "I don't recognise you. Who are you here to collect?"

"No one."

"Then you're right. You shouldn't be here." Molly's eyes darted down to the silver box. She frowned, but her eyes went to the pram. Olivia pricked up the corners of her lips. "If you're here for enrolment, you might be a little early."

"I'm here for Roxy," she explained. "Roxy Carter. Miss Carter. I'm a friend, that's all. Just dropped by to give her some support before her interview."

Molly allowed her smile to come out fully. "How kind. I'm sure she's doing wonderfully in there. Do you happen to know where this came from?"

"The workmen dug it up," she said, hooking her thumb back toward the Year One classroom. "They just ditched it here. I have no idea what it is, but there's a year engraved on it – 1990. I would have been a pupil here."

"I was in teacher training." Molly approached the box and dusted off more soil to reveal another set of numbers. "'To be opened in 2090.' Looks to be a time capsule."

"Time capsule!" Julia clicked her fingers together. "That's why it's familiar. I think I put something in it – 1990 would have been my final year here."

"In any case, they've dug it up seventy years too

early. Amir?" Molly called down the corridor, waving to a man in dark green overalls. "Do you know why this time capsule has been dug up?"

"Time capsule?" A man with soil-covered hands approached from behind Julia, nodding at her before looking down at the box. He had thick greyed hair and expressive bushy brows. Judging by his name badge, he was Amir Fallah, the groundskeeper. "My, oh my. I never expected to see this thing again. I dug the hole for it way back when."

"Apparently, it's just been found where they're digging the foundations for the new bathrooms next to Miss Carter's classroom." Molly checked her watch. "Cleaners are going to be coming down here any minute. They're not going to be able to buff around this thing."

The doors to the reception area opened, and Roxy emerged looking as downtrodden as when she'd left her classroom. Could she be finished so soon? She didn't seem to notice the muddy box captivating the Year Six teacher and the groundskeeper.

"Hell's bells!" a scratchy voice cried. "Where'd that thing come from?"

Walter Harkup, the headteacher, appeared behind Roxy. At first glance, the man who'd taught her when she'd been a Year Three student had barely changed. His shoulder-length hair was still jet black, his yellow shirt and red cardigan combination looked like he hadn't altered his wardrobe in three decades, and his coarse voice was just as grating. He only had to take a few steps into the corridor's bright light for the deep lines covering his cheeks and his hair's grey roots to emerge. He seemed to have shrunk, too – surprising, considering he'd been Julia's shortest teacher. Seeing his face had never made her feel older. He'd been around her age when he'd taught her, and yet he'd seemed old to her back then.

"A time capsule from 1990, Dad," Molly explained, folding her arms as she shook her head down at the thing. "I knew the record-keeping was bad around here, but whose idea was it to build the new bathrooms on top of it?"

"1990, you say?" Mr Harkup squinted at the box. "That's the year your mother..."

Mr Harkup's voice trailed off as he moved in closer. Further up the corridor, on the other side of the double doors that led to the upper years, the floor buffer rumbled nearer.

"Should we re-bury it somewhere else?" Molly suggested. "It's been unearthed seventy years too early."

"Students might want to see inside before you do that," Roxy suggested. "What do you think, Mr Harkup? A good idea?"

"Hmm," he grumbled, glancing as the buffer pushed through the doors. "In any case, it can't stay here. Amir, get the other side."

"I can help."

"Step aside, Miss Carter!" Walter's scratchy voice had a surprising boom. "Amir, on three. One, two, *three!*"

Neither of the men was young, but at least Amir was well-built. He hoisted the box to a decent height, but Walter Harkup could barely lift the thing off the ground. Still, he struggled as they walked toward the stage, leaving another dirt trail for the cleaners to deal with.

"On three," Walter croaked through a strained breath when they reached the stage. "One, two—"

Walter Harkup didn't reach three. He let out a groan as one hand went to his lower back. He held on for a fraction of a second before the capsule slipped from his grip. The metal box hit the tiles on the corner. Amir tried to steady it as a clunk rang through the hall, but he lost his grasp too. He jumped back as the box toppled, landing flat on its lid.

"Dad! Are you hurt?" Molly rushed in. "I think you need ice."

"I'm *fine.*"

Walter tried to straighten up but let out another almighty roar, both hands rushing to his back. He flapped his finger in the direction of the corridor, and Roxy hurried forward.

It was an odd time for Julia to remember what she'd put in the time capsule, but the detail wriggled free of its own accord. She'd handwritten and illustrated a small recipe book with her mother's help. She hadn't doubted putting it into the capsule as an eleven-year-old, but three decades later, having remembered its existence, she'd suddenly like to see it again.

"On three," she said to Amir. "One, two, three."

The time capsule lid cracked open as they lifted, and for a split second, Julia thought she might get her wish. Something fell out, but her handwritten recipe book was nowhere to be seen as a mass wrapped in plastic rolled onto the tiles.

"Uh-oh," Olivia remarked.

Uh-oh indeed.

Julia pulled the pram out of view of the sheet and, more importantly, the skeletal hand poking out through it. She hoped it was a prop left over from a long ago Halloween party, but from the shared horror on Roxy and Amir's faces, she knew they weren't going to be so lucky.

3

*H*ugging herself against the wind on the doorstep of the café, Jessie stared at the spirals of smoke rising from the blazing bonfire. The villagers, unrecognisable in their hats and scarves, had finally started to leave their homes as soon as the first whiff of smoke reached Jessie's nostrils at the café.

Peridale had a sixth sense.

Everyone knew exactly what was happening at all times.

Two people who weren't joining the flow were Dot and Percy. In their fur coats that made them look like yetis, they cut across the village green on a straight line from their cottage. Their dogs, Lady and Bruce, trotted at their feet, wearing matching red jumpers.

"Like moths to a flame!" Dot called, flinching as a firework popped off somewhere near Peridale Farm. "When will these explosions end? I can't stand this time of year."

A handful of residents glared in Dot's direction, though Jessie was holding in her laughter. She'd long since learned that her great-grandmother was best enjoyed when she wasn't taken too seriously, despite how earnestly – and often dramatically – she delivered what Julia called her 'observations.'

"It comes around but once a year, my love," Percy, her husband, assured her as Jessie stepped back to let them into the busying café. "Granted, they have been going off for weeks, but we'll hear a lot less of them after tonight. No Julia?"

"She's half an hour into a ten-minute break. The place filled up as soon as I thought about closing."

"You need the customers," Dot said as she shrugged off her fur coat. "You've been empty all day."

"Binoculars at the window again?"

"Someone has to keep an eye on this village." Casting her gaze around the café, Dot sank into one of the few empty chairs at the table occupied by Evelyn, the owner of the bed and breakfast. "We'll have two of whatever is hottest. I need thawing out."

Jessie made up two of her maple and cinnamon

hot chocolates and added them to a tray with two takeaway cups filled to the brim with squirty cream.

"Fresh from the Alps via Peridale," Jessie said before picking up the cream. "And two doggy cappuccinos. I noticed Mum took the 'No Dogs Allowed' sign down."

"And rightly so." Dot tickled Lady's head as the Maltese politely licked up the cream; Bruce, the French bulldog, was lapping his up like he was on a time limit. "Better behaved than most people's children. Absolutely decadent hot chocolate, by the way."

"Decadent. I'll take it."

"We've been watching a lot of *Countdown*," Percy whispered. "It's been quite the vocabulary expander."

"We have to do *something* with the days." Dot sighed as she fluffed up her short grey curls. "Afternoon television is the peak of excitement for me. Aren't you terribly bored, Evelyn?"

"Not at all," Evelyn replied. "Now that the B&B has quietened for the year, I finally have time to meditate as much as I want. It's been quite a treat."

"I tried that once," Dot said. "Far too much sitting around in silence for me. I prefer action."

Jessie knew Dot was hinting about the now-defunct neighbourhood watch group they'd started while she'd been away. Julia had been part of it, as had

Evelyn. Given how hard they were dodging Dot's hints lately, they had no interest in joining Dot and Percy in picking up their binoculars any time soon. As much as Jessie shared Dot's feelings on the monotony of village life, she wasn't about to start keeping watch at the window either.

"Where is your mum, anyway?" Dot asked, consulting her watch. "It always gets busy on bonfire night."

The back door to the cafe opened.

"That'll probably be her now."

Leaving the table before Dot could ask Jessie's opinion on the neighbourhood watch situation, Jessie walked into the kitchen. She expected to see her mum, so she was surprised to see her dad.

"That was quick. Was your stalkee at his office?"

"He was." Barker glanced at the beaded curtain, and Jessie noticed drops of sweat glistening on his forehead despite the cold. "I've just had the strangest phone call from a potential new client."

"How strange?"

"He's just found his ex-wife in the village. He thought she lived in the Scottish Highlands."

"Judging by the look on your face, I'm guessing he didn't find her at the station fresh off a train with a bag full of shortbread and Irn Bru?"

"She's dead," he whispered, leaning in closer, "and

she has been for thirty years. I was the first person he called."

"That is strange."

Barker retreated to his basement office to await his potential new client. Sirens drew Jessie back through the beads. Outside the café, flashing blue lights lit up the night as police cars crawled past. The gawking crowd weren't in a hurry to clear a path. Dot was already at the window. Everyone else was watching from their chairs, though the appearance of the police had hushed the conversation, which had revolved around fireworks and marshmallows in the fifteen minutes since the café reached full sitting capacity.

"Can you see where they're going, my love?" Percy asked.

"Bonfire, by the looks of it." Dot craned her neck, her nose almost pressed against the glass. "Hopefully to shut down this ridiculous event. It's been four hundred years since Guy Fawkes and his cronies tried to blow up parliament. Time to move – *Ah!* There's Julia."

A white crime scene investigation van rolled through the path cleared by the police car as Julia walked past the café window with the pram. She pulled Olivia up past the top step, and Roxy followed her in. Olivia was the only one with any semblance of a smile on her face.

"You look like you've just seen a ghost," Dot announced as the door closed behind them. "What's going on? Do you know where the police are going?"

"I think I have seen a ghost," Roxy muttered, frowning at the floor with a blank expression. "The police are going to the school. They just dug up a box."

"A box?" Dot echoed. "What kind of a box?"

"A time capsule," Julia replied. "There was a body inside it."

"A *body*?" Evelyn gasped, clutching at her jumble of crystal necklaces. "Oh, dear. That puts this afternoon's tea leaves into perspective. I've had a strange feeling all night."

"Yes, I'm sure." Dot glanced at Evelyn with a purse of her lips, though her attention returned to Julia, who wore the same blank expression as Roxy. "A body in a time capsule? When was it buried?"

"1990," Julia said.

Thirty years ago.

"Who was it?" Dot asked.

"It could have been anyone," Julia said, her brows tensing. "They were just bones."

Jessie cleared her throat. "I might know something. Was there a woman who lived in the village thirty years ago who people thought moved to the Scottish Highlands?"

Roxy gasped. "How did you know that? That's who I thought I saw."

"She's psychic!" Evelyn announced. "I've always sensed that about you, young Jessie."

"Well?" Dot demanded, hands on her hips. "Roxy? Who are you talking about?"

"Julia, do you remember Miss Campbell?" Roxy asked, to which Julia nodded. "Felicity Campbell. I'm almost certain it was her."

"How could you tell?" Julia whispered.

"She'd always wear those black turtleneck shirts with those colourful skirts. There were scraps of fabric..." Roxy's voice drifted off as her hand went up to her neck. "She was our Year Six teacher. She went missing around Christmas in 1989."

As the gossiping started up, Jessie left through the back door. Her dad's potential new client was growing all the stranger, and she had intel for him. She'd wanted a dash, but this was a whole bucket – or time capsule – more excitement.

Behind the counter, Julia sipped peppermint and liquorice tea with shaking hands. The clock had long since ticked past closing time, but the café was still filling up as word of the discovery at the school spread around the village. With fireworks blasting off all over, it would take more than her favourite tea to settle her nerves.

"It feels like too much of a celebration."

"It's as good as," Dot said, which garnered a few curious looks. "Think about it. She's been in that capsule for thirty years, and she wasn't expected to be found until 2090, when we'd all be long gone, *including* whoever put her there. She's been found seventy years ahead of schedule."

"Sound logic, my dear."

There was a murmur of agreement around the café, and Julia could see her point, even if she didn't feel like celebrating.

"I don't remember the last time I saw her," Julia thought aloud. "One day, she was there, and then she wasn't."

"I remember the last time I saw her." Roxy took a deep gulp of the latte Julia had loaded with sugar. "It was the day of the 1989 production at the end of November. *Little Red Riding Hood*. I was the grandmother. My favourite school memories come from being in those plays. Miss Campbell was there for the afternoon matinee but wasn't there for the evening show. It was the final performance, and nobody could get in touch with her. We were all so upset that she'd bailed on us after all the months we'd spent rehearsing."

Roxy wiped away tears as they tumbled down her cheeks, and Julia choked back her own. She remembered the play. She hadn't been a part of it – too shy as an eleven-year-old to get up on stage – but she'd helped paint the sets. Miss Campbell had been one of her favourite teachers, yet she hadn't given her much thought in the thirty years since she last saw her.

"She could have died that very day," Dot said, breaking a brewing silence. "Search parties all over the village were looking for her. I was part of them."

"We all were," Percy said. "I met her once when I performed magic at the school for the kiddies. She was lovely."

"Always pleasant to me when I'd go into for activities," Dot agreed with a fiddle of her brooch. "I don't remember what happened to end the search. If she's been dead all this time, why was it thought she'd been living all the way up in the Highlands?"

"She was Scottish," Julia said, remembering Miss Campbell's thick accent. "Maybe it was assumed she'd gone back home when she wasn't found? We had a new teacher when we returned to school after the Christmas break."

"Such a tragedy," Evelyn exclaimed. "She had the

loveliest long hair, as vibrant as clementines, and she was as sweet as one. To be buried in a time capsule with everyone thinking you're missing or living in Scotland is cruel beyond reckoning."

"Why do I remember her hair being short?" Dot asked.

"She shaved it off," Roxy said.

"For charity." Julia remembered the assembly where another of the teachers had clipped Miss Campbell's hair down to her scalp. Her bright smile shone through the fog of her memories. "I can't remember what charity it was—"

The door to the café opened, and for the second time that day, Julia saw Walter Harkup. She was sure he'd never ventured into the café before despite the school's proximity. His warm-coloured clothes contradicted his dragged-down lips and tensed expression. He glared around the café with a familiar look of contempt as he pulled in a wheezy breath, showing off jagged bottom teeth.

"What are you all staring at?" he called, with the same forced authority he'd had at the school. "Having a good old gossip? I have nothing to hide. I won't be anyone's scapegoat, not then, not now, and not ever." He stared around the café, but nobody rose to challenge him. "Can someone point me toward Barker Brown's office?"

Julia held a hand behind the counter. "This way."

As Walter Harkup shuffled through the café, glaring at those brave enough to hold his stare, her memory wriggled free another detail. The same point rumbled in the café's whispering.

Miss Campbell had once been Mrs Harkup.

Julia pointed him to the vestibule door that led to the basement office. Mr Harkup cleared his throat and banged down on the wood. Julia could only think how bizarre it was that he was here to see a private investigator this soon after their time capsule discovery.

Did he anticipate an arrest before morning?

Staring out at the fireworks decorating the sky above the field behind the café, Julia searched her memories for any animosity. Felicity had reverted to her maiden name before she was Julia and Roxy's teacher. The further she scanned, the blurrier the details became. But in the present moment, the pieces sharply in focus already made her scratch her head.

The missing teacher believed to have been in Scotland.

The metal time capsule she'd been hidden in for thirty years.

The ex-husband who'd immediately contacted a private investigator.

Ingredients for a puzzling case.

Closing the back door, Julia's eyes landed on her trial cake. As trivial as her earlier anxieties felt in the wake of the discovery, she already had a challenge on her hands.

The case was Barker's, after all.

4

*J*essie took the stairs two at a time before Barker could rise from his leather chair behind the mahogany desk that claimed centre stage in the windowless office. She answered the door to an old man in whacky clothes, with a mop of black hair that looked too dark against his wrinkled face.

"Barker Brown?" he demanded.

"This way," she said, stepping to the side. "I'm his ... apprentice."

Jessie followed the funny little man down the stairs and into the office where Barker had just finished kicking all of Olivia's toys under the chesterfield sofa. He gave Jessie a quizzical look she knew meant 'what are you still doing here?', but before he could ask her to leave, she busied herself making them both coffees while the pruned toddler of a man rushed through his story at break-neck speed. She laid the cups of coffee on coasters before leaning against the record player. It had been turned down, making the hazy jazz sound like it was coming from another room.

"Let me get this straight." Barker consulted the notes he'd bashed out on his laptop. "You work at the school, and—"

"I don't just *work* there. I'm the head*master!*" he corrected. "And tonight, a time capsule was dug up that contained the body of my ex-wife."

"Less than half an hour ago?" Barker checked his gold watch, a gift from Jessie for his forty-second birthday the previous day. It had been a treasure of a find from the local charity shop. "And your first thought was to seek the help of a private investigator?"

"The *very* first thought. And you're not the first I've employed either, so any funny business tactics won't work on me."

From the grit of his jaw, Jessie could tell her dad was wondering if this case would be worth it. She hoped he'd take it because she was intrigued by the weirdness of it all so far.

"Why are you so sure it was her?" Jessie asked.

"Because I *saw* her. I was married to the woman. The dates line up."

"And this time capsule?" Barker looked at his screen. "It was buried when?"

"Aren't you writing all of this down? The final term of 1989 was spent gathering items from the students to be buried, and the plan was to bury the capsule during the first week after the new year. I didn't see the thing go into the ground. I checked the records before I came here, and there was nothing related to the time capsule. Are you taking the case or not? I'll be paying in cash."

Walter reached into his pocket and tugged out a roll of shiny twenty-pound notes held together by a rubber band. The thickness of the wad made Jessie's eyes pop. Was he that sure the police would suspect him? He placed the money on the edge of the desk, almost sliding off his chair in the process. In the giant chair, his feet didn't quite reach the floor. Could this man have even picked someone up and put them in a box? He looked like he'd snap if he tried now.

"I still need some more details from you, Mr Harkup," Barker said, and Jessie could tell he was trying his best not to look at the money. "Can you go over the events of your ex-wife's disappearance from your perspective?"

"I saw her in the staffroom the morning of her

play," he said, sighing as though recounting the memory was an inconvenience. "We didn't say a word to each other."

"Not on speaking terms?" Jessie chipped in.

"We were divorced." He shot a scowl at her. "Mutually so. That never helped my case the first time around. The play was on the last Friday of November, and she was reported as missing when she didn't turn up for work on Monday. Nobody ever came forward to say they saw her after that Friday. The police hounded me for weeks. The interviews, the searching, the constant prodding and poking made my life a living hell. When the letters finally cleared things up—"

"Letters?" Barker interrupted.

"They arrived in the first week of 1990 with Scottish postmarks. Flick grew up in Scotland, so it made sense that's where she'd run to."

"Flick?" Jessie asked.

"Oh." Walter's brows dropped, and he seemed caught off guard. "Felicity's nickname. It's what we called her. People close to her. Flick moved down from Scotland during her teacher training. That's when I met her. I thought she was too airy fairy to make a good teacher, but we got stuck in a lift together. It was only for a few hours, but it felt like we were there for a lifetime. We got to know each other, we were married the following year, and we had our daughter the year after that. It all moved quite quickly."

"How did you go from that to not speaking to each other?" Jessie asked.

"Because *adult* relationships are complicated, girl." His frown deepened at her. "Flick loved nothing more than a project, and I think she saw me as another project. I grew up in the army. I understood that children need firm instruction and discipline to succeed, and to her, I was a boulder to soften."

"These letters?" Barker pushed, his fingers typing. "How did they 'clear' things up? Who sent them?"

"Felicity sent them," he said, his voice quietening. "At least, that's what we thought at the time. I was as convinced as everyone that she wrote them. The handwriting looked like hers, and her confession was enough to quell the police investigation."

"Confession about what?" Jessie asked.

"Stealing the charity money. That's why it was so easy to believe she'd run away after we received the letters. She raised thousands by shaving her head for a children's hospital charity. She looked so different, so I was never surprised that the Scottish police never found her. I thought she'd taken the money and started a new quiet life elsewhere. If I'd known she was here ... right where I worked ... for all these years ... I ... I ..."

Walter plucked a tissue from the box on Barker's desk and blew his nose like he was playing the trombone.

"She shaved her head in the summer of 1989, and the money went missing soon after," he continued. "She accused almost everyone of taking it. The hair-shaving raised the most, but it was quite extreme. I thought she was doing it to get back at me."

"Get back at you for what?" Jessie asked. "Sounds to me like she did it for a good cause."

"For the divorce. She knew I loved her hair. It was what first attracted me to her. She looked frightful after her head was shaved."

Jessie wanted to call him shallow, but she bit her tongue. From the little she'd heard of Felicity Campbell, she couldn't fathom what a man like Walter Harkup could do or say to charm such a nice-sounding woman.

"Were you one of the people she accused?" Barker asked.

"Yes, I was," he snapped, dabbing at his eyes with the scrunched-up tissue. "That was the year Mr Perkins left, and we'd both applied for the role of headmaster. She accused me because she thought I was trying to ruin her reputation, but I'm as innocent now as I was then, and this is finally my chance to prove it. I'm to retire this year, and I've felt the shadow of doubt looming over me for three decades. I won't spend what precious time I have left rotting in a cell for something I didn't do. My innocence must be proven, so are you to take the case or not, Mr Brown?"

Jessie looked at her father, who was finally taking in the wad of cash on the desk. Large deposit or not, she couldn't believe he was considering his options. This case was too juicy to pass up.

"I will try my best," Barker stated. "Being her ex-spouse, the police *will* pull you in for questioning. There's no doubt about it. Be honest and stick to the facts. This isn't going to be a local police case. They will bring in cold case specialists, and they won't leave a stone unturned. I'll try my best to turn those stones too, but I don't have access to the resources they do. Cold cases are difficult enough at the best of times, so I need to be the first person to know anything you remember."

"I've told you the little I do know."

"The letters?" Jessie prompted, pushing away from the sideboard. "I'm going to assume you didn't receive multiple, so we'll need the names of the other people she accused."

Jessie plucked a pen from the pot on the desk, and Barker slid across a blank sheet of paper. Walter scribbled down four names before sliding off the chair.

"Can I leave you to get started, Mr Brown?" he said as he dropped the pen back with the others. "I promised my daughter I wouldn't be too long, and as you can imagine, she's quite distressed at the discovery of her mother."

"If you remember anything at all—"

"I have your number," Walter called over his shoulder on his way to the staircase. "Prove my innocence, Mr Brown, and there's more money where that came from."

Walter left the office. Jessie sat in the still-warm chair and sipped the coffee he hadn't touched. Barker arched his brows at her over the list of names.

"My apprentice?"

"I asked some valuable questions, didn't I?" Jessie nodded at the paper. "He'd have left without giving you those if it wasn't for me. Do you think she sent those letters from Scotland?"

"If she did, she came back to the village afterwards to die." Barker pinned the piece of paper on his green investigation board. "I'd say it's more likely that one of these five people took a little trip up North to 'quell the investigation', as dear Walter put it. Because if she left to start a new life with thousands in stolen charity money, why would she have bothered to accuse anyone?"

"You were right, this is strange, and it's getting

stranger by the second." Jessie pulled out her phone and tapped the desk. "Let me look at those names. Might as well start by seeing who our suspects are."

Later that night, at her cottage on the outskirts of Peridale, Julia pulled the blanket up to Olivia's chin. Her eyelids were twitching up a storm. Hopefully, she was having sweeter dreams than the reality in the village. Word had spread to every corner, judging by how busy the café had been when Julia finally closed. She stayed open for as long as she could, but when Olivia fell asleep in her pram, she flipped the sign and announced that everyone could return tomorrow.

Friday was sure to be a busy day. The café always proved to be the perfect spot for gossip and a slice of cake on a small news day, but someone as well-loved as Felicity Campbell was sure to keep the seats filled. From the night's stories, she and Roxy weren't the only ones who had loved the teacher. She'd touched many lives in her years teaching. The only black spot on her reputation was the accusations of the stolen money that had leaked into the conversation from multiple angles.

After Barker clarified Walter's version of events,

she was in no doubt that the black spot was part of a cover-up.

"Look at you," Roxy whispered as she peered over Julia's shoulder into the cot. "You're a natural. Is it as knackering as people say?"

"Absolutely." Julia accepted a cold glass of wine from Roxy. "But it's worth it. I have one to look after. You have twenty."

"Twenty-eight," Roxy corrected, yawning. "And I get to send them home at the end of the day. Honestly, I think you're all mad. I can't handle a goldfish. Won't be long before those two are expecting."

Leaving Olivia sleeping soundly in her cot, Julia and Roxy joined Leah and Johnny in the sitting room. The soon-to-be-married couple were snuggled up in Julia's favourite armchair by the fireplace. Julia and Roxy took the sofa. Leah had come to ask about the cake after spending the day in Oxford with a client for whom she was planning a wedding. Despite Johnny being the newspaper editor, Julia had been the one to break the news to Leah. She hadn't stopped crying since she'd sat down. Johnny followed soon after with a camera full of pictures of the school and a notepad full of 'no comment' responses.

"It's just such a shock," Leah explained, accepting a tissue from Johnny. "I can't believe she was there all this time. How could someone do such a thing to her?"

"Weren't Campbell and Harkup both in line for the headteacher job?" Johnny speculated with a scratch of his dark curls. "That's a good enough motive for me. His name is all over the paper's archives. He was the number one suspect until those letters arrived. I read a quote today from Miss Spencer, our Year Two teacher, who went on record in 1989 saying she caught them in a blazing row days before Felicity went missing. I can't imagine Miss Campbell in an argument with anyone."

"Me neither," Leah said. "She was such a good teacher. So kind-hearted."

"She helped me with my stutter on lunchbreaks," Johnny said. "I didn't even realise it as a kid, but she gave me speech therapy without me knowing. Kids were always pointing it out."

"Remember when Miss Campbell tripped over and poured that glass of water on me during our mock maths exam?" Leah said, barely above a whisper. "She only did that because I had a little accident, and she could see I was too embarrassed to put my hand up. I was so stressed about getting it perfect."

"Some things never change then, Wedding Planner Supreme." Roxy toasted her wine glass. "Miss

Campbell would always give me a role in the play even though I could never remember my lines. She had the patience of a saint. From being on the other side, it isn't as easy as it looks. Kids will test your patience on every level."

"I always used to bake for her," Julia added, creeping closer to the fire as the logs finally erupted from the simmering kindling. "I only baked for the teachers I liked. Harkup never got so much as a biscuit."

"She was one of the good ones," Leah said. "Somebody has to do something. How can we go ahead with the wedding with this looming over us?"

"Steady on, Leah," Roxy said. "You're not going to cancel the wedding over this. They might have already solved it throughout this conversation. I bet they've already matched a spec of DNA to the animal that did this. And if not today, tomorrow. There are still three weeks to go."

"Two weeks and two days."

Julia's stomach knotted, and she sipped more wine. She'd been rounding up to three weeks too. Was it really that close? The week had blurred by already, but she agreed with Leah. How were any of them supposed to focus on anything other than what was happening with Miss Campbell? Even if they didn't do anything, the constant stream of news – or lack of it – would keep them on edge.

"I'll keep digging through the archives to see if there are any details that could help," Johnny offered. "And I heard Walter has hired Barker?"

"Wants to protect his own back," Roxy said with a huff. "I saw him searching for 'private investigators in Peridale' on his phone before he told us to leave. Doesn't that look dodgy to anyone else?"

"I never liked him," Leah said. "Always a misery guts."

"I can report he hasn't changed," Roxy said. "I'll keep my ear open at the school when it opens again, and so will Julia at the café, won't you?"

Julia smiled and nodded that she would, but her foot was already tapping. Could she sit around waiting for something to happen, a wedding cake to design or not? Swirling the wine, she let what Leah had said spin around her mind. Miss Campbell *had* been one of the good ones.

"Her legacy deserved better," Julia said, raising her glass. "To Miss Campbell and to a quick resolution."

The four toasted, and they continued to share their memories of Miss Campbell for the next hour. The yawning started when they ran out of Miss Campbell memories and ventured into more general childhood reminiscing. It didn't take long for Leah and Johnny to excuse themselves. Once they left to return to Leah's cottage across the lane, Julia checked in on Olivia while Roxy was topping up their wine in the kitchen.

"I never asked." Julia leaned against the breakfast bar as she looked through to the bottom of the garden, where a small fire was flickering. She could just about make out a silhouette. "How did your interview go?"

"Oh, it was an absolute nightmare," she said, throwing the bottle into the recycling box with a clink. "Harkup basically told me I didn't stand a chance. Totally crushed me, but it was only the worst thing that happened today for a few minutes."

"A body falling out of a time capsule will do that."

"I wonder what happened to all the stuff we donated for the capsule. I wrote a letter. Can't remember what it was about. Hardly important now, is it?" Hugging herself, Roxy gazed through the window to the fire. "You think Barker can figure this out?"

"I don't doubt it."

"Let's hope so." Roxy put her wine down and sighed. "Don't suppose I can kip on your sofa tonight, mate? I'm not feeling sleeping in the flat alone."

She almost asked about Violet but remembered that Roxy had said she was away for a 'family thing.'

"Sofa is yours."

"Cheers. Can I have a shower? I haven't felt clean since that thing burst open."

With Roxy in the shower, Julia pulled on her coat. She took her wine to the bottom of the garden where Barker had started a fire in the metal wastepaper bin that usually lived next to his office desk. He was toasting marshmallows on a stick.

"Didn't want to miss out," he said, patting the log next to him. His fingers brushed against an open packet of giant white marshmallows. "Find yourself a twig. They're helping with the thinking."

Julia found a twig amongst the curled leaves decorating her back garden. She sat next to Barker on the log, and he shared his blanket around her shoulders. With three marshmallows crammed on, she leaned them over the fire. The fluffy flesh caramelised to a satisfying golden crisp.

"That's how savages eat marshmallows," Julia said as Barker bit into his. "Hasn't anyone ever shown you the proper way? You're supposed to peel it off layer by layer."

Julia demonstrated with a pinch of her fingers. The top skin pulled away in gooey trails, and she dropped it into her mouth. For something so simple, it was delicious.

"You learn something new every day. Thanks for the lesson."

Julia let the silence sit for a moment. When Barker didn't bring up what he'd been thinking about alone at the bottom of the garden, she cleared her throat. "Speaking of lessons—"

"Nice segue."

"Thanks." She laughed, peeling off another crackled layer of the shrinking marshmallow. "How's the investigation going? Jessie mentioned that Mr Harkup gave you a list?"

"You *can* call him Walter," Barker said. "Not that he seems to like it."

"I'm not sure I can. He'll always be Mr Harkup to me. Mean Mr Harkup. I never liked him."

"No, he wasn't the most amiable man. Jessie didn't seem to like him much either." Barker peeled off a layer of marshmallow after refilling his stick. "My turn for a segue. How are things with Jessie in the café at the moment?"

The change of direction surprised Julia.

"Fine, I think? Has she said otherwise?"

"No, but she did employ herself as my apprentice today. Unpaid apprentice. She's rather eager to assist me on the case. I could tell her to cool off if you need her in the café?"

"No," Julia answered immediately. "If she wants to

help you on a case, she's old enough to make that decision, and I'd be a hypocrite to say otherwise. I want in, Barker."

"Are you sure?"

Julia nodded, and rather than peeling off a layer, she took a big bite.

"I just spent the night listening to stories of how much people loved her. Her legacy needs to be put straight, and I don't think I'll be able to sit by and do nothing. The names? Suspects?"

"According to Walter, he was one of five people sent one of these mysterious letters. Interviewing each of them is the logical place to start. We need to find out their relationship with Felicity, why she accused them, and when was the last time they saw her. If she disappeared without a trace on November 24th, 1989, someone would have been the last person to see her." He pulled out his phone and scrolled to a note. "The only people who have obvious connections are Walter and Molly Harkup, the ex-husband and the daughter. There's Daphne Nation, who runs the café at the Fern Moore estate; Amir Fallah, the groundskeeper at the school; and Liberty Turner, who we haven't been able to track down."

"Amir was at the school tonight," Julia pointed out. "He mentioned that he dug the time capsule hole.

And I think I might be able to set something up with Molly through Roxy."

"Then we're off to a good start because this won't be easy. DI Christie is still under review after blundering the Electric Fury case. I haven't had sight nor sound of him since, and I saw who they've brought in to head the cold case investigation when I was locking up earlier. Detective Inspector Laura Moyes. She's tenacious. She'll rip this village apart to find the truth if she has to."

"Good," Julia agreed, tossing her finished stick into the fire, "because Miss Campbell needs the best. This won't be easy, but my gran made a good point earlier. Miss Campbell might have been in that capsule for thirty years, but we've opened her up seventy years before we should have. Someone out there has lived for thirty years thinking they've got away with murder. I imagine this has turned their world upside down, so all we need to do is pay attention."

5

*O*ver breakfast, Julia, Barker, and Roxy listened to the news bulletin on the radio between the usual optimistic pop songs they blasted every morning. Even Olivia stopped her bouncing to listen to the solemn reporter's confirmation.

"The body found recently in a time capsule at St. Peter's Primary School, in Peridale, has been confirmed to be that of a former teacher, Felicity Campbell, once the subject of a missing person's case dating back to the final months of the 1980s."

The café didn't take long to fill up. After such a rare late opening the previous night, Julia felt as though she'd barely left the place, but after a few espresso shots, she was alert enough to serve with Jessie by her side. Roxy did an excellent job babysitting at the cottage, thanks to the closed school. However, the emergence of a stubby molar through Olivia's gums kept Julia occupied with teething rings and settling a wailing almost-one-year-old for the rest of the night.

Saturday burned by like Friday, and with no new information to discuss, the same stories spun around in what Jessie had likened to 'being stuck next to the person who won't stop talking through the flight, but it's the same story, and you're flying to Australia.'

When Julia's eyes opened with the late rising sun on Sunday morning, she was glad for the chance to change that. It took Molly all of Friday to return Roxy's voicemail about meeting with 'someone from Barker Brown, PI's office.' When Molly called, she enthusiastically set up an appointment at her home for Sunday at lunchtime. With Roxy still camping out on the sofa, Julia and Roxy set off to Riverswick a little after eleven, leaving Barker home with Olivia. So far he'd had a door slammed in his face by Daphne Nation at her café in Fern Moore, hadn't been able to track Amir Fallah down with the school being closed, and still hadn't been able to locate Liberty Turner.

"Turn left up here," Roxy said, tapping the dash as they drove down a road of large, detached houses. Julia turned into a quiet cul-de-sac. A bright yellow police car disrupted the peaceful golden hues of the

Cotswold stone cottages with their prim and proper gardens, barely a fallen leaf in sight. "If I remember correctly, that's Walter's house the police are parked outside. Molly organises a Christmas party at her house every year, and I don't think anyone dares not go. There's no official deputy headteacher role, but if there were, she'd have it, and with her dad being the head ... how do you not go to that party? Every year, Walter shows his face, takes a single lap of the room handing out Christmas bonuses, and then lurches back to his house without so much as a goodbye. They're always so incredibly dull and very polite, and then everyone sees themselves out one by one, and we meet at the nearest pub without the higher-ups."

"Barker said the police have been interviewing him every day. They're putting pressure on him. You should have heard Walter screaming down the phone last night at ten o'clock because Barker hadn't cracked the case."

"Can't say I'm surprised that Walter wants a thirty-year-old case cracked in three days. If he wants it, he wants it yesterday. And anything to save his skin. In my first year working under him, I dared ask him if he'd eaten the cinnamon roll that I'd left wrapped up in a napkin on the side. He went on a rant about how dare I accuse him and who was I to question his integrity in front of the other teachers and blah blah

blah. Made me feel this small." Roxy pinched her fingers together with a sliver of a gap. "He had cinnamon roll crumbs around his mouth and down his tie – everyone saw them – and they all stood by and said nothing. I'm not saying I'm harbouring a grudge, but if Barker could add that to the case, I'd be thrilled. Missing cinnamon roll." Her finger drummed on the dashboard. "Write that down. Besides, I could hear Walter through the walls when I brushed my teeth in the bathroom. My ears are too delicately tuned to that ranting voice of his. I never realised how quiet you had it up by the farm. Mulberry Lane can turn rancid after midnight. I'm sure half my neighbours live in the pub. Speaking of which, did you bring up the hen party to Leah?"

"Didn't feel like the right time."

"No, you're right. If this isn't wrapped up, we can't let this drag Leah down. I take my responsibilities as bridesmaid seriously. I saw her out pruning those rose bushes in her front garden this morning, and she looked dead behind the eyes. It was quite unnerving."

"Maybe I can cheer her up with some cake samples later," Julia thought aloud. She hadn't had time to take another stab at her autumnal decorating experiments. "We're right on time. Let's not keep her waiting."

Julia climbed out of her aqua blue Ford Anglia as

another car entered the cul-de-sac. Its metallic skin was a shivering grey with a brilliant sheen. It glided like liquid metal to a silent stop behind the marked police car. A tall woman with hair as gleaming as the vehicle climbed out. She wore a maroon blouse and pencil skirt under a near-pavement-grazing beige coat, the tones complementary to her dark blonde hair. Her eyes were trained on Walter's house as she slammed her car door. On her way to the garden path, she glanced at Julia's car, and her tight mouth lifted into a half-smile.

"How adorable," she said, her voice soft and husky. She clicked her key over her shoulder, and her car beeped as it locked. "Love the colour."

"Thanks."

Judging by her lack of uniform and the conviction in her steps as she walked up to Walter's house, Julia assumed she had just met Detective Inspector Laura Moyes.

Sundays in Peridale always moved slowly, but in her small flat above the post office, Jessie's fingers were anything but sluggish as she typed on her phone. With her mum taking Molly and her dad tracking down Liberty, she had opted to find Amir. She'd dropped in at the school at different points over the last few days with no luck, and she couldn't imagine the groundskeeper working weekends even if the school hadn't been closed.

School had never been Jessie's favourite place to be. She'd failed all her high school exams. Her only qualification was a level 1 patisserie and baking certificate from her brief college stint during her early days at the café. College had been the first time she'd enjoyed education, and with Julia guiding her behind the scenes, she'd excelled in the practical side of things. However, she'd struggled with the paperwork every time. She still didn't know why she'd needed to do so much writing to learn to bake, but that side hadn't come naturally to her.

If only she'd been given an exam in tracking people down on the internet.

That, as she was finding out, she was good at.

She typed in the phone number she'd found on the Fallah and Sons' groundskeeping and landscaping company's website, which boasted that its clients included St. Peter's Primary School, Hollins High School, and Wellington Heights. She'd found the website by cross-searching a picture of Amir, which she found on Hollins' website and not St. Peter's.

As the phone rang, she knew she'd only have one stab at this.

"Fallah and Sons," a woman answered. "How can I help you?"

"Hi, I hope you can help me," Jessie said, injecting a drop of panic into her voice as she paced her flat. "I'm a project manager at Wellington Heights, and I've locked my calendar in an office that isn't going to be opened until Monday. Can you believe it?" She paused for a breath. "My boss will *kill* me if I don't confirm the upcoming schedule, so it'd be a huge help if you could just confirm when the next appointment for groundskeeping services is booked in for."

"Wellington Heights, you say?"

"Mmhm."

Jessie bit her tongue before she prattled on. She'd given her best impression of one of the many businesspeople she'd heard in many airports worldwide. No matter the country, someone in a suit would be talking too loudly on their phone, stressed about something.

"Today at three," the woman said. "Is there anything else I can help you with?"

"That's exactly what I thought. You've been a great help."

Jessie hung up with a grin.

Suspect found.

Molly welcomed Julia and Roxy into her home. The décor was a little dated, but everything was neat and orderly. She showed them into the sitting room, where a black and white cat slept in a rocking chair by the window. There was a basket of wool and whatever Molly was working on rested on the chair arm in a bundle of stitches and knitting needles.

"Did you knit your cardigan yourself?" Julia asked. "You were wearing one like it at the school on Thursday."

"Ah, yes, we have met," Molly said with a nod. "I thought you looked familiar. You were the lady with the sweet little girl in the pram. Yes, I did knit it."

"It's lovely," Julia said. "I've never given it a go."

"Just a little something to pass the hours, not that there are many free hours in a teacher's life, which I'm sure Roxy can attest to. Make yourselves comfortable, and I'll go and make a pot of tea. Excuse the mess."

Julia almost asked 'what mess' until she saw the archway leading to the dining room. A mountain of documents consumed the dining table, and empty drawers hung from the cupboards lining the walls. Julia and Roxy settled into the sofa, and Molly hurried in with tea and biscuits.

"I've spent all morning looking for *this*," Molly said, pulling a clear plastic folder from the mantlepiece. "I knew I'd kept it. The police were here before they went to my father's, and they took the original, but I made you a copy. I thought it might help with your investigation."

Molly handed over the clear wallet and scooped up her cat. "Come on, Betsy." It settled limply back into her lap.

Julia pulled the letter from the sleeve and read:

To my darling Molly,
Blaming you for the missing money will always be my biggest regret. I hope you can forgive me. You'll never have to see me again. Forget about me.
I love you.
Mum

"I went to look for her." Molly stared out of the window, though her gaze was further away than the house across the street. "On four separate occasions. I assumed she didn't want to be found. I gave it one last stab when I turned forty. That's how old she was when she left ... when I *thought* she left." She stopped stroking the cat and stared down, her brows pinching into a deep line above her nose. "All these years, I've wondered what happened to her because of that letter. The police say it could be a forgery, and she never left the village. They're saying she likely died November 24th, 1989."

"The day of the play," Roxy confirmed. "When did you last see your mum?"

"That afternoon. We met up for lunch in The Plough. I wanted to wish her luck with the autumn production. She'd worked so hard on it, and I couldn't make the performances. I was juggling teacher training and a part-time job in a factory at the time."

"You managed to have another job when you were training?" Roxy said as Molly poured herself some tea. "When did you find time to sleep?"

"I've always enjoyed keeping busy, and life as a student didn't come cheap, even back then. We were at the pub between a quarter past three and four, a detail the police confirmed in 1989 with witness statements and bar receipts. We had fish and chips, and a glass of champagne each to celebrate her play. I've gone over that day so many times, thinking maybe I'd missed something. That there was some clue or hint that she was about to leave."

"And this letter convinced you of that." Julia read over it again, questions brewing. "You'd know your mother's handwriting, so this must be convincing if she didn't write it?"

"Even now, I can't tell it's not hers." Molly glanced

in the direction of the letter, but she didn't seem to be able to focus on it. "If it's fake, they did a good enough job to fool me. It fooled everyone."

"Why do you think she accused you?"

"She accused everyone," she said. "Me, my dad, my cousin."

"Your cousin being?"

"Libbie." Molly rocked in the chair, and the cat slinked off to the ground, letting out a yawn and stretching out its claws. "Libbie Turner. She lived with us at the time. My mum's sister, Auntie Ada, sent Libbie down from Scotland. Ada died a few years ago. I last saw her in the early days of Mum being missing. That's the first place I checked on my first search up there. The years pass far too quickly." She sipped her tea. "Ada thought my mum could straighten her out because she was a teacher, but she struggled just as much. Libbie turned everything upside down. She was always thieving and lying. When she was charged for stealing the charity money, it was easy for us all to believe."

"She was charged?" Julia asked.

"The money was kept in a lock box that my mum kept in her school desk, and they found the smashed open box in Libbie's rucksack when she was caught shoplifting. My mum was devastated. After the divorce and the threat to her reputation, I thought that was the end of her bad times. As broken as she was, she'd started to level out again. The play had given her something to focus on."

"Miss Campbell never gave away that she was dealing with all this stuff," Roxy said quietly. "She was always such a ray of sunshine."

"You know what it's like as well as I do. Good teachers shouldn't take their problems to school, no matter what. My mum was a consummate professional. She loved teaching. She's the one who inspired me into the profession. When she accused me, it broke my heart."

"Were you close before the charity money?" Julia asked.

"Incredibly close. We'd do everything together. She'd let me help mark her students' work for practice, and I'd go on weekends to help with her classroom displays. I learned so much from her. I wished I could have been at St. Peter's when she was. We could have put on a play together. I carried that on for her. For the part of me that never stopped loving her, even though I believed that letter for so many years."

Molly turned away and stifled back tears. Roxy plucked a tissue from the box next to a pile of unopened parcels that looked like online shopping and passed it toward the rocking chair. She knocked over a stack of letters and quickly bent to pick them up. On her way, she shuffled through the pile; it was all seemed to be junk mail.

"I get tons of this stuff, too," Roxy said.

"Drives me crazy." Molly was seemingly glad to talk about something else. "I'm probably never going to change my internet, get another credit card, or sell my house." The tears took over again. "This isn't the sort of closure I thought I'd get."

"We'll do what we can," Julia assured her with a smile. "Is there anything else you think might help us?"

"Well, now that I've just said everything about Libbie, with a new light being shone on these letters, I can't help but wonder if she *did* take that charity money after all. She always denied it, but as I said, she wasn't the most honest of people. She took my things, money from Mum's purse, and never admitted it."

"Do you know where I can find her?" Julia asked, sensing that Molly's energy for questioning was fading now that the tears weren't stopping.

Molly shook her head. "No, sorry. I haven't seen her in years. She'll be a couple of years older than the two of you. She was fifteen back then." Molly rose from her chair, her eyes going back to the window. "Looks like the police are finished, and I have a casserole to try and feed to my father. He's barely eating. They're harassing him more now than they did then. I hate to see this put on him."

"We'll get out of your hair," Roxy said as she stood, taking a couple of biscuits from the untouched plate. "If I can do anything, you have my number, Molly."

"Thank you." They hugged. "And if anything happens, Julia, keep me updated. If I think of anything else, I have the number for Mr Brown's office."

Carrying a casserole dish wrapped in cling film, Molly showed them to the door and followed them out. She crossed the cul-de-sac, nodding at the police officers and DI Moyes on her way. To Julia's surprise, the DI approached them.

"Are you two friends of the family?"

"I work at the school with her," Roxy said. "And Julia runs the café. We were students of Miss Campbell."

"Then I'll say I'm sorry for your loss." Her tone was flat, as though she'd uttered the phrase hundreds of times. "Julia South-Brown, isn't it? Wife of the former DI? Though from what I've heard, you're much more than that. Your reputation precedes you."

"It's probably only half true," Julia said. "But as does yours."

"Really?" DI Moyes flashed a sceptical smile. "What do they say?"

"That you're tenacious."

"Hmm. I thought it would be worse." She rocked back on her heels before clicking her car key. "I won't tell you what they say about you at the station, but I get a funny feeling that they're all a little afraid of you. I'm sure we'll be seeing each other around."

DI Moyes climbed into her car and was the first to leave the cul-de-sac.

"I can't tell if she was being sincere," Julia said as she shoved the key into the slightly rusty lock of her vintage car, "or incredibly sarcastic."

"I'm glad you said it."

6

"Where are you sneaking off to?"

The question caught Jessie by surprise. She tugged her flat door shut and smiled at Dot, who was leaning against the post office wall wearing an outfit Jessie had never seen before. Trousers, for one, with a matching jacket that made her usual white collared shirt and brooch look less fuddy-duddy. A copper-hued beret was tilted on her grey curls. All that was missing was a cigarette on a stick.

"Digging the look, Dorothy. Who says I'm sneaking off to anywhere?"

"Forget my outfit. You're the one wearing *sneaking* clothes." Dot tugged Jessie's cap down over her eyes.

Rather than pull it up, Jessie tilted her head and looked out from under the rim. "You're helping Barker with his case. Don't try to deny it. Your mum too. I called the cottage. Barker is home alone with Olivia. There hasn't been a Sunday in the previous seven that Julia hasn't been at home."

"And I thought *I* needed to get out more." Jessie tucked her arm through Dot's, and they set off down the alley. "Yes, I'm helping Barker, and obviously, so is my mum. The time capsule woman was her teacher. And yes, you can come with me. I'm not the only one in a sneaking outfit."

Dot tugged at the jacket. "Do you really like it?"

"I love it. You look like you're on your way to liberate an old people's home or something."

Jessie filled Dot in on what they'd found out so far as they made their way to Wellington Heights, which had been Wellington Manor before Jessie left the village. A billboard sporting bright images of luxuriously decorated apartments greeted them next to the new gates enclosing the development.

"I hear only one has sold so far," Dot whispered as they kicked through the leaves covering the gravel driveway. The scaffolding-smothered sandstone building came into view, the manor a looming presence on the horizon. "And that was from the owner, James Jacobson, to his son, Richie. I'm pretty sure it doesn't even count because Daddy James definitely paid for it, just like that new bar."

"I'm surprised you didn't protest a bar opening on your doorstep."

"I *was* tempted, but it's quite pleasant there. Percy and I sometimes wander over for a tipple when the evenings drag on. I saw Walter in there last night, drowning his sorrows. He caused *quite* the scene. Tried starting fights with anyone who would look at him. Ranting about just having come from another police interview. If he's innocent as he claims, he's not painting a great picture of himself."

"Which is why we need to focus on the bigger picture. Walter paid my dad to prove his innocence, not me. I want the truth regardless of the outcome, and I'm not sure I trust Mr Headmaster."

"Then maybe this groundskeeper can help us. Is that him?"

Dot cast a finger around the side of the house where a young man was digging a trench against the manor.

"Too young. I think that's one of the sons. Leave this with me."

It looked like whatever he was digging would soon be a flower bed, though there wasn't a flower to be seen around the building site that had swallowed up the grand house. Tucking her hands into her pockets, Jessie ran up to the guy. He stopped his digging and looked up at her.

"Hi there, so sorry to bother you. You see that woman over there?" Jessie pointed to Dot, peering through a window that used the go to the kitchen. "That's my great-grandmother, and she's got more money than sense. She's thinking of buying one of these apartments, but she won't stop asking about the gardens. Are you in charge around here?"

"No, but I can tell you the plans."

"She's very *particular* about speaking to the person in charge." They both looked to Dot as she wiped her finger along the glass and rubbed the grime between her fingers, unknowingly playing along. "Old people, right?"

"Right." He unclipped a walkie-talkie from his belt and called, "Dad, you're needed at the house."

Jessie retreated to Dot before Amir's son asked more questions. Amir, a man in at least his late sixties, emerged from the thick forest with a large wheelbarrow full of chopped wood. It took him several minutes to make his way to the manor. He handled it efficiently, and it wasn't difficult to visualise him single-handedly burying a time capsule. His son whispered something to him, and he approached with a cautious look.

"Can I help you?"

"Hi, I'm Jessie, and this is my great-gran, Dot." Jessie outstretched her hand. "I just told your son a small lie to get you here because I wasn't sure if he would have called you over if I said I was here today representing Baker Brown, PI."

"Both of us are," Dot cut in. "On Walter Harkup's orders."

"You're here now," Jessie said, rocking back on her Doc Martens. "So, it would be awesome if you could answer a few questions."

"Okay," Amir said with a shrug. "I have nothing to hide. I was just about to take a break anyway."

From Roxy's flat window above the candle shop at the top of Mulberry Lane, Julia looked down Peridale's oldest shopping street to her stepmother's nail salon. The shop, like the street, had the usual Sunday quietness, but it gave Julia an idea.

"Why don't we take Leah to get her nails done?" Julia called over her shoulder as Roxy packed more clothes in the flat's only bedroom. "It can be a practice for her wedding set."

"Considering how many dress fittings she's had us do, I think she'll love that. Good bridesmaid points."

Julia quickly sent Katie a text message to book the appointment, and while her phone was in her hand, she opened the web browser. She typed in her question and waited.

And waited.

"If you're trying to get a signal, you'll be waiting awhile," Roxy said as she crossed from the bedroom to the bathroom. "It's shocking on this street."

"Trying to figure out how easy it is to forge someone's handwriting so well that it could convince a daughter and an ex-husband."

"Molly was right about students only seeing certain sides of teachers, but even so, I find it difficult to swallow that they all accepted the letters. It doesn't seem like something she'd ever do, regardless of what was going on in her life. You can hook up to my Wi-Fi or use my laptop. I shouldn't be too much longer."

The Wi-Fi router was on a table behind a pile of clothes that flowed over from the mountain in front of the washing machine at the edge of the tiny kitchen. Julia opted for the laptop. She picked it up from the coffee table covered in books open on pages of unsure handwriting. It looked like Roxy's Year One kids had been learning to double and halve numbers. It wouldn't be long until Julia was helping Olivia with her homework. She sat in the middle of the low sofa and peeled open the laptop on her knee.

An application form greeted her on the screen. It had half been filled in with what looked like Roxy's work experience. Julia scrolled to the top. A job application for a school. A school in Liverpool. Julia glanced at Roxy, who was stuffing clothes into a backpack. Liverpool was at least a few hundred miles away. Hours outside of commuting distance. Was Roxy planning on leaving the village? Julia parted her lips, but the question didn't make its way out. She went to a fresh window, clicked on the search bar, and typed in her question.

"Says here that forging someone's handwriting is 'difficult but not impossible'," Julia read aloud from the summary at the top of the page. "With enough samples and time, it could be done."

"Teachers are always putting their pen to paper, so the samples wouldn't have been difficult to get hold of."

"And so far, she was last seen in November 1989, but the letters didn't come from Scotland until after the new year. Would two months be enough?"

"It was only a couple of sentences," Roxy pointed out. "I was expecting reams and reams, but it was condensed. Might as well have said, 'I'm sorry, I did it. Goodbye.'"

"Good point." Julia nodded her agreement as Roxy emerged from the bedroom with her rucksack. "Ready?"

"Should be enough for a few days. Are you sure you don't mind me kipping on your sofa for a bit longer?"

"Of course not."

"I know I'm being a big baby about it all, but I don't want to be alone. Most of my dreams end up at the school somehow. I spend most of my time there, so that part makes sense. But now Miss Campbell keeps popping up in them. Keeps waking me up."

"Explains why I heard a teaspoon rattling around in a cup at four this morning. We need to change the song in your subconscious by setting the record straight. Molly pointed us at Liberty Turner. Don't suppose you've heard the name?"

"Can't say I have, but I'm sure if you ask enough people in the café tomorrow, someone will point you in the right direction. For now, when was the last time we wasted a Sunday in the pub?"

Julia placed the laptop back on the workbooks, and she couldn't recall.

"Your silence says it all," Roxy called, already on her way downstairs. "First round is on me."

On her way, Julia glanced back at the laptop. It had been too long, and she'd drifted further away from her friend than she had realised. Once upon a time, she'd have heard about any notion of moving away as soon as it crossed Roxy's mind. As much as she didn't want to think of such things, Julia hoped she wasn't losing her friend so soon after their lives had re-synced.

The sweeping staircase and crystal chandelier made the entrance hall of Wellington Heights feel almost as it always had done. The familiarity faded as Jessie followed Amir through a door built into a wall where the kitchen archway had once been. The windows were in the same places, but that's where the similarities ended in the once grand kitchen. A wall cut the room in two through where the impossibly long marble island used to command attention, creating a white box that looked like it would make a spacious living room. They followed Amir down a bright corridor, past equally spacious bedrooms and a bathroom, to another open area at the back. A kitchen had been built around the French doors looking out to the never-ending lawns.

"For the prices they're trying to sell them for," Dot said with a wrinkle of her nose, "you could buy a whole house."

"It is a whole house, it's twice as big as my flat, and it used to be one room."

Amir filled a kettle at the sink, the tea and coffee-making station the only items in the blank canvas box. He threw a teabag into a cup and didn't offer them anything. Jessie suspected they wouldn't have long. She remembered the list of questions Barker had prepped her to ask if she tracked him down, but she decided to start somewhere else.

"I heard you dug the hole for the time capsule?" Jessie asked.

"I did, and it wasn't where those builders dug it up. The hole I dug was at the front of the school, and I helped them lower a capsule into it after the Christmas and New Year break. The second capsule, that is. Like Flick, we thought the first had gone missing, so Mr Perkins, the head at the time, had another box made."

Flick.

The nickname Walter had used.

"You were close with Felicity," Jessie stated.

"Yes." He nodded before taking a sip of tea, his gaze distant. "I came to this country as an asylum seeker in the early nineteen-eighties during the conflicts in my home country of Iran. I spoke some basic English but couldn't write anything except my name. It wasn't an easy language to pick up as a

Persian. When I started working at the school, only Flick gave me the time of day. She was the only person to give me a Christmas card during my first year here. I sent her one back written in Persian, and that's when she offered to teach me to write. She was the busiest teacher in the school, but she always made time for our lessons. It's hard to spend that much time with someone and not grow close."

"She still accused you when the money went missing," Dot said bluntly. "Why would she do that if you were so close?"

"I wasn't the only one." His distant gaze snapped onto Dot, the accusation in her voice not going unnoticed. Jessie wondered if she'd made a mistake by not coming alone. "By the autumn of 1989, my written English was good enough for me to apply for a small business loan. Working at the school, I used what they provided to do my job, but I had a lot of free time during my days. I knew I could grow a business if I owned a van and some equipment. I fled war for an opportunity, and the loan gave me that. I've been able to put my four sons through university, and I owe that to Flick's kindness in giving me the time that she did to teach me. But the loan couldn't have come through at a worse time. I was approved the day after the charity money vanished from her desk. I bought my van, and I was the second person she accused."

"Who was the first?" Jessie asked.

"Walter." He took a short sip of tea. "I think that's where most people's minds went at the school. Those paying attention, at least."

"Why was that?" Dot said.

"Because he was trying to sabotage her. They'd both applied to be the head, and Felicity was the better teacher for the job. There was no way she wasn't going to get it. The charity money went missing the day before the governors announced their decision. The money paused everything and put Flick under a huge amount of stress. Not just to find the money but for the sake of her reputation. I heard teachers whispering that she might have taken the money herself, and that someone close to her had all but confirmed it."

"Do you think that person could have been Walter?" Jessie asked.

"That's where my mind went back then. I knew Flick hadn't written the letters, and Walter was the first person I thought could be behind them. He wanted Flick out of the way. He never forgave her for the divorce."

"You thought the letters were fake?"

"How could they not be?" Amir checked his watch and looked at the glass doors. "I said as much to the police back then, but they didn't believe me about that any more than they believed me about that child's mother smashing the window."

"What child's mother?" Dot pushed.

"Kyle Nation. He was a troublemaker, and his mother blamed Flick for his expulsion. She kept confronting Flick at the school gates, trying to start fights. It was harassment. Not long after the play finished, I heard smashing glass coming from Flick's classroom. I ran to the scene, and the kid's mother was running away. Flick was nowhere to be seen."

"Would that mother be Daphne Nation?" Jessie asked.

"That's her. The police didn't charge her despite my statement. She called me a liar, and nobody else came forward to say they saw her, but I knew it was her. She had a ring in her eyebrow."

"Why were you so sure the letters were fake?" Dot asked, picking up on what he'd said. "They were good enough for the police."

"I only saw mine, and it looked the part, but it didn't sound like my Flick had written it." He paused, his brows dropping. "It was like it had been written by a stranger who had no idea about our relationship."

"Relationship?" Jessie echoed.

"Friendship," he corrected quickly. "Friendly relationship. Look, there's still a lot to do before this place is ready for the spring, and I've already lost enough time with all the police interviews over the last few days."

Amir tossed his tea down the sink and made for the doors to the garden. What was it Barker had said to find out about? Their connection to Flick, why they were accused, and...

"There is one more thing," Jessie called as he opened the door. "When did you last see Flick?"

"About two hours before the evening performance of the play," he said. "Around five. I was raking leaves, and I saw her run across the playground. I waved to her, but she didn't see me. Her eyes were streaming."

"Do you know why she was crying?"

"I never got the chance to ask," he said, bowing his head as he glanced over his shoulder. "Now, if you'll excuse me, I told you everything I know."

On their way out of the manor, Jessie plucked a brochure from a stand near the front door. She flicked through as she went over everything Amir had just said, but Dot was the one to articulate what was going through her mind.

"I think he was closer to Felicity Campbell than he was letting on," Dot said as they set off back down the driveway. "He didn't need to backtrack when you picked him up on using 'relationship', but he peddled quicker than the Wicked Witch of the West in a twister."

"I noticed that too."

"And he seemed to know the ins and outs of Flick's divorce. Hardly a student and teacher relationship."

"That, I didn't notice. Nice spot."

"These apartments do look rather fancy," Dot said, taking the brochure from Jessie to flick through. "Percy and I floated the idea of selling the cottage and maybe moving into one to see what it's like living in a slice of a manor at least once before we die. Not sure we'll get there."

"Given these prices, I don't think I'll ever be able to afford anything around here."

"Maybe not on your own. You won't be young and single forever, and there's always Alfie. You could go in on something together for investment's sake."

Strangely, it had been something they'd spoken about during their travels. Alfie had been the one to bring it up when they'd been in a tiny apartment in Tokyo. Being a builder by trade, he'd suggested they could both chip in on something small and renovate it to get their feet on the property ladder. When she'd left him in Japan, he'd assured her he'd be home by Christmas. Now they had half a world between them, Christmas was around the corner, and neither of them had brought up the topic of his return flight yet.

"Maybe one day," Jessie said, tucking the rolled-up brochure inside her jacket. "But here and now, Amir

Fallah has pointed his finger at Daphne Nation, who I already know runs the café at the Fern Moore estate. If Amir was telling the truth about seeing her, there's a chance she was up to more than smashing windows on the last day anyone saw Felicity."

---

7

*J*ulia was relieved when she woke to a still room on Monday morning. It had been spinning a little too much when she'd finally made it back to the cottage after her afternoon in the pub with Roxy turned into an evening at Richie's Bar.

"Did I make a fool of myself last night?" Roxy groaned as she hugged a cup of coffee at the breakfast bar. "I have scratches on my arm."

"You fell sideways out of the taxi and over the wall into Leah's rose bushes." Barker poured a coffee from the French press and pushed it to Julia as she sat next to Roxy. "It was apparently the funniest thing Julia had ever seen. I haven't seen you laugh like that in a long time."

"I'm glad you were amused by my misfortune," Roxy said.

"Johnny and Leah chimed in from their bedroom window," Barker said. "And so did I, for that matter. You rolled out and tumbled up to your feet like you were in the circus."

"You were always the class clown, Rox." Julia sipped her coffee gratefully.

"Oh, no school." Roxy let out a sigh of relief and toasted her coffee. "I'll drink to that. Miss Campbell saves the day. What were you saying about bacon sandwiches, Barker, and do I have time to go for a shower?" Roxy sniffed her hair. "I smell like garlic, and there's a taste in my mouth I can't quite put my finger on."

"That'll be the donner kebabs you came home with," Barker said, pulling the bacon packet from the fridge, "Which, rather impressively, stayed in your hand during your tumble."

"I'll add 'acrobat' to my CV."

Once Roxy was in the shower, Julia made Olivia's breakfast of porridge oats and sliced banana sprinkled with cinnamon while Barker fried the bacon.

"Are you okay with Roxy staying here for a few more days?" Julia asked. "I think she's going through something outside this Miss Campbell situation."

"Fine by me. She's entertaining, and she's helping out with Olivia. Always feels like there's an extra pair of hands needed. What's going on with her?"

"When I was at her flat yesterday, I saw her applying for a job in Liverpool. She interviewed for the headteacher job at St. Peter's, and Mr Harkup told her she didn't stand a chance. I think she's craving some change, and I don't think it's come out of the blue." Leaning across the breakfast bar, Julia whispered, "When was the last time you saw Violet? She's apparently away for 'family stuff', but at Roxy's flat yesterday, it was like she'd been living there alone for a while. Her stuff had taken over the place. I hope I'm wrong because if I'm right, Roxy has chosen not to tell me. We've known each other since we were in single digits. I should have been there for her."

"Friendship is a two-way street, Julia," Barker said as he slathered butter on slices of wholemeal bread. "Roxy hasn't made much effort with you since Olivia came along, and she turns one at the end of the month."

"Regardless," Julia said, looking to the bathroom. "The only two people in my life that I've known longer are my dad and my gran. Before I was friends with anyone – Johnny and Leah included – I was best friends with Roxy. It'll take more than a few years of distance to change that." She sipped her coffee. "But speaking of Leah and roots, I hope the café isn't too busy this morning because I'm meeting her for a nail appointment at lunchtime, and she's inevitably going to want to see what I've been working on. I haven't nudged the needle since before the time capsule."

"Murder cases will do that." Barker sliced a sandwich down the diagonal before putting it on a plate in front of Julia. "You'll need your strength. We both will. I'm going to take another crack at Daphne at Fern Moore, and I still need to track down this Liberty Turner. Going off what Molly said, Liberty will be up there with Walter on the police's suspects list." He pulled his phone from his dressing gown and sighed. "Speaking of the devil, he still hasn't returned any of my calls from yesterday. I don't know how he expects me to solve this case with his walls up as high as they are. Makes me wonder what he's hiding." Barker took a bite from his sandwich, and a dollop of brown sauce fell from the end. "I know he's a strange man, but hiring a PI would be more than strange if you were guilty, wouldn't it?"

"Strange and stupid."

"Makes him look innocent, but it would take a clever mind to fool a PI and the police." Barker thought for a moment. "Or someone who *thought* they were clever enough to pull it off. Either way, he's paying me to figure this out. If he doesn't want to answer his phone, he's only wasting his time."

After finishing her breakfast, Julia wasted no more of her own time in driving to her sister's cottage to drop off Olivia for a day with her cousins, Dottie and Pearl.

"I never had Miss Campbell as a teacher," Sue said during their brief doorstep conversation. "But Mr Harkup was my headteacher, and let's just say, I wouldn't have been sending the twins there if he was still there in a few years."

"Seeing how things are going, it'll probably be his daughter."

"Miss Harkup was my Year Two teacher, but you'd never know they were related if not for the name. If the way people have been talking about Miss Campbell these last few days is true, she definitely took after her mother when it came to teaching because she was lovely."

With a promise that she'd pick up Olivia once the workday was over, Julia headed to the café. When she had rows and rows of cakes baking in the ovens for the day ahead, she peeled the leaves off the sample layer. She gathered her equipment and a handful of carefully selected leaves plucked from the village green.

If she'd brought in the real thing last time, she'd

have known she needed to make them thinner from the start. She rolled out a sheet of white fondant icing, and using the same leaf cutters, she cut out half a dozen shapes. She pulled chunks off a couple to make them more irregular and smoothed out the edges so they'd curl better. After creating veins with a toothpick, she laid them over different-sized cans and jars to dry.

"They're looking crispier already," Jessie said when she rolled into the café from her flat next door, ten minutes before opening. "They look pale, but I'd say you've cracked it."

"We'll see." Julia tilted her head. "I'm thinking of using coloured dusting powder instead of food colouring to build up the shades a little better. The second attempt is better than the first, at least. Something to show Leah today. If you're fine on your own, I need to go out for an hour. It's the only time Katie could fit us in for a wedding trial."

"Mondays are always quiet."

Except for this one.

Given how Julia had almost needed to force people out of the door at the end of Saturday, she should have known it would spill over to the following week. With how quiet the village's news cycle had been since the police's initial statement, the inhabitants of Peridale were as hungry for answers as

Julia. Dot was happy to share with her audience, as always.

"You should have seen the groundskeeper squirming under questioning," Dot announced as she paced around the full café. "Sweat was pouring down his forehead, and his hands were shaking so much he was practically throwing his tea around the room."

"That never happened," Jessie whispered behind the counter.

"There's another time capsule buried somewhere at the school for which *he* dug the hole." Dot's finger wagged above her head. "Easy to envision him digging a second hole, don't you think?"

Dot's proclamation set jaws off wagging. Noticing the time, Julia bid Jessie goodbye and left with her boxed samples. Usually, she would never have left Jessie with such a full café, but Dot wouldn't let her captive audience go to waste. She'd no doubt still be talking on Julia's return.

Julia drove to Mulberry Lane, which was keeping the usual Monday calm to itself. She parked outside of Katie's Salon and saw the back of Roxy's head on the other side of the pink neon sign.

"Leah's not here yet," Roxy said, sitting on the white leather sofa and flicking through a magazine. "Wedding emergency. Said she'd get here when she could."

"Emergency?" Katie, Julia's stepmother, gasped behind her desk as she filed a customer's nails. "Nothing serious, I hope?"

"Knowing Leah, her dress will have needed taking in a few millimetres, or the florist cut the sample flowers half an inch too short. Please tell me you've brought me something delicious again. That bacon sandwich barely touched the sides."

"Only a box full of edible leaves," Julia said, cracking the box to show the collection in their kitchen roll swaddling. She was rather pleased with how they'd turned out this time. "And they're only for looking at. Wanted to get Leah's thoughts and hopefully ease her mind about the wedding cake."

Julia joined Roxy in flicking through magazines for the next twenty minutes while Katie finished her customers' nail. After the woman paid and left – leaving a shiny five-pound note in the tip jar on her way out – Katie joined them at the sofas.

"Is Leah going to be much longer?" Katie whispered. "I could only block out a little time. I'm booked up back-to-back all week. Word has really started to spread."

"I've only been hearing good things," Julia said proudly. "You've taken the village by storm."

"You know what else is taking the village by storm?" Katie leaned over and pulled something glossy from behind the acrylic reception desk. "Brochures for Wellington Heights. Ready for spring, apparently."

Julia assessed Katie's expression, which was always a little frozen thanks to her 'dentist trips', but she didn't seem as affected by seeing her ancestral home sliced up into apartments as Julia thought she would.

"Wouldn't it be funny if your father, Vinnie, and I ended up back there? Another few years of the salon's books looking like they do, and we might be able to afford a mortgage. Wouldn't that be quite the turnaround?"

"They are pretty nice," Roxy said. "I went for a viewing at the one they've finished. I think it used to be your kitchen."

Katie's smile wavered for a moment, but she continued flipping through the pictures.

"Jessie saw that one too," Julia added. "Said it looked huge."

"That room was always too big." Katie tossed the brochure down on the magazines. "That whole house was. This way, tons of people can enjoy it. What was Jessie doing there, anyway? She's a little young to be tethered by a mortgage."

"She went to talk to the new groundskeeper. He's connected to the teacher in the capsule case, and

Barker's been hired by the prime suspect. Have you heard about it?"

"Have I *heard* about it?" Katie chuckled. "I used to think the café was the only place people liked to gossip, but I hear everything here. People get quite candid when their hands are in mine. I keep joking with your father that I should take some therapy courses next. My latest certificate just came in, so if either of you needs a wax, let me know." She winked. "Oh, and Julia, I think it's about time I thread your eyebrows again."

"Oh, I'm good, for now." Julia scratched at the side of her head as her cheeks heated up. Her brows had only finished growing back after Katie's September threading string attack. "Don't suppose you've heard anything interesting about the case?"

"One customer last night and two more this morning think the groundskeeper did it," Katie whispered, looking around her empty salon. Julia wondered how many people her gran had called already. "Is it just Barker, or are you—"

"Julia's all over it," Roxy cut in. "Who was that woman you were looking for? Maybe she's one of Katie's clients."

Katie sat upright, looking excited at the chance of being able to help.

"Don't suppose you know a woman called Liberty?" Julia asked. "Liberty Turner?"

Katie shook her head. "No, sorry."

"Worth a shot." Roxy shrugged. "She'll turn up."

"Not Liberty," Katie continued, "but I know a Libbie."

"Molly called her 'Libbie'," Julia remembered. "She said she was fifteen back then, so she'll be ... mid-forties?"

"Yeah, about that." Katie nodded to the window. "She works in the charity shop across the road. I got quite friendly with her when the money troubles first started. It was the only way to keep up, what with Vinnie outgrowing everything monthly."

Turning in her chair to stare through the neon sign, Julia could make out the small charity shop. She smiled, feeling like a game of hide and seek had just ended. Almost ended. She checked her watch and hoped Leah's wedding emergency was nothing too serious. It wasn't like Leah to be late.

"And he had these *gigantic* hands," Dot cried, far too long into her uninterrupted rambling. "Hands so big you could really see him burying a box on his own with little trouble."

The back door opened, and Jessie turned expecting to see her mum, but again, she was surprised to see her dad. Pushing through the beads, she joined him in the kitchen, where he was twirling around a leaf Julia had left.

"I see she's cracked it."

"Those are the rejects," Jessie said. "I don't think she'll be satisfied until it looks like she's rolled the cake around in the forest. You don't look delighted, either. Mum said you'd gone to talk to Daphne?"

"I attempted to talk to Daphne, but she kicked me out of her café again and told me if I came back, she'd set her son on me." Barker tugged at his tie. "And I still haven't heard from Walter. I wish he'd left an address."

"Mum'll know where he is. She said he lives across from Molly's house. Maybe the police have arrested him and haven't made the announcement yet?"

"That would make things easier." He sighed. "I'm beginning to think this case is leading me nowhere but dead ends."

Jessie wasn't so ready to give up. While Barker made himself an americano at the coffee machine, Jessie visited the social media page where she'd previously confirmed that Daphne ran Fern Moore's café. She tapped on the opening times tab. Open until six. Jessie would have half an hour to get there, and Daphne would have had the rest of the day to calm down after Barker's visit. She'd seen him interviewing people before. He couldn't help but switch back into his old detective inspector tone, which was packed with enough forced authority to scare certain people into silence.

Some people needed a different approach.

The Jessie approach.

When Katie's next client turned up, Roxy and Julia left with apologies for wasting her time. They each dropped a fiver into the tip jar on their way out.

"I'm starting to get worried now," Roxy said, her phone at her ear outside the salon. "She's not answering her phone. It's not like Leah to forget something like this. I should go and check to see if she's at home."

Roxy left with a promise that she'd let Julia know when she found Leah. Julia crossed the road to the charity shop, not wanting the trip to Mulberry Lane to be wasted. A woman with an abundance of beaded jewellery around her neck and wrists was sign-writing large red letters, advertising an 'AUTUMN SALE'. On the other side of the door, Julia realised the woman, who seemed to be in her mid-forties, was writing the letters backwards.

Rather than launching straight into her questions, Julia scanned the aisles. She rifled through the baby clothes and toys, though her eyes kept going to the woman at the window, who was equally keeping an eye on her. Moving to the second-hand cooking section, Julia offered a smile that wasn't returned. Molly had been easy to talk to, as had Amir, according to Jessie, so she hoped she wasn't about to be stonewalled. She picked up a couple of pots, absentmindedly lifting their lids. Her fingers touched purple silicone, and finally, something caught her attention.

Julia looked down at a silicone mould in a familiar shape. Lifting it in two, the inside had a delicate stamp of a leaf, so perfect it looked like it had been fossilised in stone. She pulled her boxed samples from her bag and cracked the lid. They wouldn't do. It was a find so unique she was glad she hadn't had the chance to show Leah her latest samples.

"This is exactly what I need," Julia said when they met at the counter, glad of something to say. "I run the café around the corner."

"Never been." She thrust the mould into a bag. "Three quid. You know, if you're the police, you have to tell me. Don't think I didn't notice you staring at me. You work for that Moyes woman?"

Libbie's Scottish accent was still there, although softened by her decades spent living so far south of the border.

"No, but my husband is a private investigator looking into what happened to Felicity," Julia admitted. She hoped her honesty would dampen the hostile edges. "Your name is Liberty Turner. Libbie, isn't it? I'm Julia. I know Katie."

"Katie who?"

"Blonde hair. Runs the new nail salon across the street."

"Oh, her. The bimbo. You don't look like someone who'd be friends with her."

"Technically, she's my stepmother, but you know as well as I do that family isn't simple."

"What do you know about anything?" Felicity slammed the till and banged Julia's two-pound coin change on the counter. Wooden beaded bracelets rattled at her wrist. "I have things to do."

Libbie moved around the corner with her head down and went to the children's toys section. Acting as though Julia wasn't there, she started digging through the box, checking over teddies before moving on to the next. None were beyond a few stitches and a spin in the washing machine.

"Looking for anything specific?" Julia asked, crouching next to her. "Do you have kids? I have two daughters."

"No." She snapped. "It's for my neighbour. Flat walls are thin. I hear the little girl crying every night. Not my business, but I dunno, I wanted to help."

"Sounds like Felicity."

"You knew her?"

"She was my teacher the year she went missing. Or should I say, the year she was murdered and buried. I'm sorry for your loss, by the way. She was your auntie? Took you in, didn't she?"

"Yeah." Libbie stared suspiciously. "Who told you to talk to me?"

"Molly."

"I should have known." Liberty forced a laugh, throwing down a stuffed giraffe. "She hated me from the minute I showed up. Flick was just trying to do her best by me. I was a bit of a wild child back then, I won't lie. But Molly made everything difficult. She hated me, and I never did anything to her. She was too used to being an only child. Couldn't stand how close I was with Flick."

"She said you stole from her and from Flick."

"Don't ever call her that. You didn't know her. She was your teacher, that's all."

"I'm sorry."

"And yeah, I did steal. I won't deny it." Libbie's voice lowered, and her eyes went down as she turned over a stuffed smiling sunflower. "I'm not proud of it. She could have thrown me out then, and she'd have had every right to, but she didn't. She gave me another chance, and I never stole off her again."

"Weren't you charged with stealing the charity money?"

"And the charges were dropped as soon as that letter arrived with the confession. I didn't take any money from any charity, but I might as well have. Flick turned her back on me and kicked me out. Said she'd never felt more betrayed in her whole life. Do you know how hard that was? I have five brothers and two sisters in Scotland, and I was the only one who was sent away. My mum died years ago, but the lot of them are still on her side about me. Doesn't matter that I straightened myself out, eventually. But of all the people ... Flick ... that hurt the most." She scrubbed tears away with her sleeve. "I stopped hating her years ago, but I really *did* hate her."

Hate her enough to kill her?

"Didn't they find it when you were shoplifting?"

"Believe me, it was the last time I ever shoplifted. I was only nicking a few cassette tapes from Woolworths. Hardly the crime of the century. They charged me without a second thought based on the empty money box. If I had stolen the charity money, why was I shoplifting in Woolworths? I could have bought the cassettes."

Libbie raised a good point, but the delivery sounded rehearsed, as though she'd said it countless times over the years.

"Look," Libbie said with a sigh, "Molly, Flick, I don't blame them for thinking I did it. I get it. I stole from them when I first moved down here, but I was used to that. It was survival. I cut it out when I realised I didn't need to anymore. I tried to get along. I knew I had a good thing with Flick. She took care of me better than anyone ever had. I've never been closer to anyone in my life, then or now."

"If you didn't take the money, who do you think did?"

"Dunno," she said, settling on a stuffed worm before pushing herself up. "Back then, I thought her ex stitched me up. I saw Walter at the house the morning I was arrested. My bag was on the kitchen table. Police were never going to believe me. He never made it a secret that he blamed me for their divorce. He said I put too much stress on them, but Flick assured me their marriage had been heading to that point anyway. I sped things up, that's all. I don't know what she ever saw in him. I thought she'd be way happier with…"

Libbie's voice trailed off as she took the stuffed worm to the counter. She tossed a coin into the till and busied herself straightening up a display of cardboard bookmarks.

"Happier with?" Julia prompted. "Was she seeing someone else?"

"I promised I'd keep it secret."

"Libbie, she's been dead for thirty years."

"A secret is a secret." Libbie sniffed, folding her arms tightly. "I need to get back to work."

"Me too." Julia glanced at her watch. "One last question. When did you last see Felicity?"

"The night before she went missing. I was out on bail waiting for my sentencing, and she came again to ask if I did it. She kept telling me just to admit it, so I told her to clear off and leave me alone. After that letter came, I thought she was trying to cover her back one last time. Made sense to me that she'd left, and at least I was let off the hook."

With Libbie dabbing at her tears, Julia didn't want to push things any further. Standing on the pavement outside of the charity shop, Julia took in the sign writing. The penmanship was impressive, especially as it had been written backwards.

"They said this would happen," a voice startled her from behind. Julia spun to see DI Laura Moyes staring over her sunglasses from her shiny car. Julia hadn't heard her pull up. Had to be electric. "You're living up to your reputation, Mrs South-Brown."

"Just Julia is fine."

"Well, Just Julia," DI Moyes said as she joined Julia on the pavement. "Once, I could believe was a coincidence, but two of my suspect interviews? There are rumours your gran has a police radio and keeps you up to date with what we're doing."

"People like to talk around here, but that's wild even by Peridale's standards. First I'm hearing about it. And no, I'm not here shopping. I came to talk to Libbie."

DI Moyes glanced at the charity shop with a tight grin. "She wasn't easy for us to track down."

"Helps when you know someone in every corner. Local intel gets you far."

"Yes, I can imagine." Moyes shook back her jacket sleeve and checked a smartwatch. "I'm free tomorrow afternoon. If your cafe is open, I'll drop by for a coffee. I'm not opposed to working with the community on this. "

"Tomorrow it is."

DI Moyes entered the charity shop, and before Julia could reach her car, her gran ran across the street.

"Thought you'd be at the café still."

"I have a nail appointment." Dot wriggled her

fingers. "Started coming to help Katie look busy, for support, but I grew quite fond of having them done, so I have a standing weekly appointment. Was that the new DI you were just talking to?"

"DI Laura Moyes. Brought in for the cold case. She seems a lot less closed off than DI Christie. She's coming to the cafe tomorrow to swap notes." Julia unlocked her car and added, "Gran, please tell me you don't have a police radio."

Dot let out a strained laugh. "I don't have a police radio. That's preposterous, ludicrous, absurd—"

"Jessie said you'd been watching *Countdown*."

Dot was already halfway across the street. "Can't be late for my appointment."

Julia almost followed to demand a straight answer, but she wasn't sure she wanted to know. Driving back through the village, she had more pressing matters on her mind. After her conversation with Libbie, she was eager to speak to Walter Harkup.

Things weren't adding up.

8

*I*n a rare moment of self-reflection later that day, the villagers of Peridale seemed to notice they'd stretched their shreds of information to the breaking point. The conversation swirled in familiar rhythms and repetitions thanks to Dot's orchestrating, but when she left for an appointment, nobody was able to capture the collective imagination quite the same. With no developments to light up the story, the moths scattered.

Monday ended as most Mondays did, quiet enough that Jessie could leave early. She caught the bus at the stop outside the post office. The bus drove up the lane toward her parents' cottage. Her yellow Mini was still parked outside. She'd yet to insure or tax it since her return, happy to use public transport.

She'd come to appreciate good public transport during her time away, and the buses through Peridale were semi-regular and mostly on time.

Johnny Watson boarded outside Peridale Farm. He paid the driver before scanning the bus. When he noticed Jessie, he took the seat in front of her. They were both on their way to Fern Moore for different reasons.

"Need to take some pictures of a family fighting their eviction after their rent soared," he said, holding up his camera. "Developers have been snapping up flats all over Fern Moore and regenerating them to double the rents. I always thought that place would be immune to gentrification."

"I thought the council owned it?"

"They do. Or that's how it started out, at least. The government's Right to Buy scheme changed that in the eighties. At least half of them are privately owned, and prices are soaring. I keep hearing people blaming the apartments at Wellington Heights for driving prices up in the postcode. Daphne Nation bought her flat, and you'll never guess in which year."

"1989?"

"Too easy, wasn't it?" Johnny leaned in and pushed up his glasses. "I've been digging through the archives to see if I can turn anything up. Daphne gave a fantastically candid interview in 1989 when Felicity went missing. She didn't hold back."

And yet Barker hadn't been able to get her to talk.

"What did she have to say for herself?"

"Quite mean-spirited things about Felicity. They were the only non-glowing comments I could find from the period she was still missing. I'm surprised my predecessors printed it, though I'm not sure I could resist either." Johnny suppressed a smile. "Daphne openly admitted that she hated Felicity for what happened with her son. She wasn't going to join in the searches because Felicity was, and I quote, 'finally getting hers.' I know Daphne owns her flat because she said that's why Felicity accused her of stealing the money. Merely a coincidence that her cash deposit was around the same amount, according to Daphne. When asked how she acquired the funds, she replied it was 'none of your business.'"

"That is all quite candid." Jessie tilted her head at the ID badge around Johnny's neck, and she smiled when she saw it didn't have a picture. "I don't suppose I could borrow that?"

The two concrete blocks of flats that made up the Fern Moore estate came into view, and they made their way to the front of the bus. They staggered to a halt and the doors shuddered open. A gang of lads greeted them at the bus stop with suspicious glares. The usual welcome.

"This place always gives me the jitters," Johnny said, looking around as they set off toward the shadow of the blocks. "Especially at night."

"Just keep your head down, and you'll be fine," she said. "This place is nowhere near as scary as people in the village make out."

"Still, don't leave without me," Johnny called across the courtyard with a wave. "I'll meet you at the bus stop."

Head down, Jessie approached the block of four shops. There'd been a café and a mini supermarket before she'd left, but the two empty units sandwiched between the two had been filled with a pizza takeaway and a barber. Compared to the quiet village she'd just left, all four were buzzing with life, and the café seemed to be the heart of the buzz despite being at the end of the row.

Maybe Daphne's Café and Julia's weren't so different.

After Julia's interview with Libbie, information from Daphne would complete the suspect set. Jessie stepped inside and joined the back of the line queueing at the counter. Unlike the cabinets at Julia's café, the focus here was savoury over sweet. Pre-made sandwich rolls bursting with meats and salad filled one side of the display, with pies and pasties on the other. A glowing box filled with thick-skinned jacket potatoes sat next to a coffee machine that looked similar to the one Jessie was so familiar with. The selection of cakes and desserts came wrapped in plastic. A glance around the full café revealed that the all-day breakfast seemed to be the most popular item. When it was her turn to be served by the eyebrow-pierced woman juggling everything on her own, Jessie ordered the same with a hot chocolate.

"Daph," a man in a flat cap called across the café. "Can I get more ketchup on my table? Bottle's run out."

"The amount you use, I'll have to start charging you extra," she called as she pulled a fresh bottle from under the counter. "And you can get off your backside and come and get it, Jeff. Can't you see I have my hands full?"

Jeff shuffled across the café, and Daphne pulled the bottle back a few times before finally handing it over. They both laughed, and the people around them offered a few chuckles as the old man lumbered back to his chair. He'd fit into the usual crowd at Julia's Café, but the gathering leaned much younger here. Mostly builders fresh from work and young mums feeding their kids dinner. Jessie heard less gossip and more people talking about their own lives.

"No use lingering around. It won't get made any quicker." Daphne glanced at Jessie over her shoulder. "Go and find a seat, and I'll bring it over."

Jessie put her coat over a chair at the least messy of the three empty tables. Using one of the trays left behind, Jessie stacked up the cups, saucers, and empty sugar packets.

"I was just about to do that," Daphne said when she came over with Jessie's order. She balanced it on her hip and ran a wet cloth over Jessie's chosen table. "Thanks all the same, I suppose."

"Sorry, a force of habit."

"I know you," Daphne stated. "You're that girl who used to go around with Billy Matthews. I live in the flat two doors down from where his mum used to live. You two still a thing?"

"Haven't been for a while." Jessie kept her expression neutral, not wanting to express how surprised she was to have her cover blown so soon by the mention of her ex-boyfriend. "Last saw him before he joined the army."

"Is he still doing that? I didn't think he could hack it."

"I'm not sure," Jessie confessed. "It's been a while since we've been in touch."

"Life is like that." Daphne pulled a knife and fork

wrapped in a napkin from her apron and placed it on the tray. "Enjoy your food."

Jessie removed the items from the tray, another force of habit drilled into her by Julia from when she'd first started working at the café. Trays went out and came straight back in because nobody needed the clutter on their table. Jessie placed it on the chair next to her and tucked it in. She watched Daphne work as people came and went. Like Julia, she was a natural at keeping her crowd entertained and attended to. Her approach was different, but it created a light atmosphere, nonetheless. And from her fry-up, the food was well made, and the prices were impossibly low for the portion size.

After finishing her food, Jessie slowly sipped her hot chocolate while waiting for an opening to talk to Daphne. She hoped she'd come around to clear more tables as people started to leave but preparing the food orders kept her busy behind the counter. Jessie cleared the table and the one nearest her and took the tray up to the counter. She placed it atop the latest issue of *The Peridale Post*, sporting the 'TEACHER TIME CAPSULE CORPSE' headline. It had been covered in cup ring marks.

"Thanks," Daphne said, a little less defensively this time. "You work in a café?"

"My mum owns one." Technically not a lie, but

not the answer to the question either. "Don't suppose you've seen Billy around here lately? I'd have thought he'd have come back on leave a few times by now."

"His mum ran off to Rotherham after some bloke," she said. "Haven't seen him around these parts. Sorry, love. Did you come all this way to find him?"

That would work.

"I did," she said with a sigh. "Just wanted to talk to him. Like I said, I haven't heard from him in a while." Daphne continued buttering a slice of toast, and Jessie knew it was now or never. "You're Daphne, right?"

"Have been for fifty-eight years."

"You're not Daphne Nation, by any chance?" Jessie dug into her coat and pulled out the ID badge. She gave it a quick flash with her thumb over Johnny's name. Daphne stopped her butter spreading. "You might be able to help me. I've just got a job at the paper. My first week, actually, and I'm pretty sure they're going to fire me. I sent the wrong article to print and ... it's a long story, but a quote from you might just get me through my trial period."

"I have nothing to say to the press," Daphne said with a bite to her voice as she scraped around the edges of the almost-finished butter box. "I can't help you."

"They dug up your quotes from 1989, and they're going to reprint them," Jessie blurted out as though it were a secret. "My editor is writing the article as we speak." Daphne's eyes darted around the café, so Jessie leaned in. "A new quote from you might help smooth over some of the things you said back then."

The panic in Daphne's eyes as she sliced the toast before sliding it onto a plate made Jessie want to admit there was no article. Still, she could see Daphne considering her options. She placed the tray on the waiting customer's table and pulled her apron over her head.

"I'll talk to you," she said. "Just not in here. The walls have ears."

Not so different, after all.

The back of the café opened onto a car park surrounded by garages and storage units. Silhouettes moved around a fire in the centre. Daphne kicked two milk crates upside down and dropped into one with a sigh Jessie knew all too well.

"You better not be trying to stitch me up like that last fella," Daphne ordered as her head leaned against the wall of graffiti'ed concrete blocks. "I've worked for years to get to this point. Now that my profits are finally in the black, the last thing I need is people looking at me funny because of something that was printed when I was twenty-eight."

"How were you stitched up? Did you not say those things about Felicity?"

"I said them, alright, I just shouldn't have said them out loud to him. He told me he wouldn't use any of it. He blew everything I said out of proportion. Made me look guilty as sin. Had the police knocking on my door."

"You said you were glad she 'got hers.' What did you mean by that?"

"Exactly what you think. I didn't care if bad things were happening to her after what she did to my Kyle. Do you know how often we moved around so he could go to new schools? St. Peter's was his last chance before they sent him to an awful school for 'problem children.' Miss Campbell knew that. I made sure she knew that. That woman had the nerve to look at me and say it was for the best, like she had the right to decide his future. If she'd given him another chance, things might have turned out differently for my Kyle. I hated her then, and I hate her now. I don't care that she's dead. In fact, I take it back. I don't care if you print this. Put it on the front page. I want people to know who she really was." Daphne paused and caught her breath. "She ruined my life. She ruined my son's life."

"I had to change schools a lot, so I know it's difficult to integrate into a class. How was Miss Campbell behind your son being expelled? What did he do?"

"He wasn't a bad kid deep down, but he could never settle anywhere." Daphne stared ahead at the fire. "He just needed some good role models, that's all. I tried my best. Between working in the car factory canteen and cleaning the nursing home, I had my hands full. Felicity grew up too comfortable to know what it's like to struggle. She would never let things drop. I can't believe I even tried to make her see sense. Stubborn, selfish woman."

Whatever Kyle did, his mother couldn't seem to face it.

"The charity money," Jessie moved on. "She accused you because you bought your flat?"

"When her charity money went missing, I was only surprised she didn't accuse me first. Claimed I was harassing her. She kept avoiding me at the school gates. I just wanted to talk. I think she thought I was going to smack her. I wanted to wipe that smug look off her face, but I held back. I knew it would only make things worse. She didn't say as much, but I knew she only blamed me because she saw me as beneath her. Classist woman, if ever I've met one. How could someone like me possibly afford a deposit to buy her flat from the council? That's what she was thinking."

"Is that what she said?"

"No, but I know how people like her think."

Daphne sucked her teeth up at the dark sky above. "Always looking down their noses at people like me."

"And how did you get that money?"

"None of your business." Daphne leaned forward and pushed herself up. "Are we done now?"

"Not quite." Jessie followed her to her feet and stood between Daphne and the door. "You were spotted at the school on the night Felicity went missing. Spotted near a smashed window."

"And I'll say now what I said then." Daphne stared down as she rolled a stone under her shoe. "The groundskeeper needs his eyes tested because I was nowhere near the school."

"Off the record," Jessie whispered, leaning in, "but I heard another witness has come forward saying they saw you there. You might as well admit it. They'll not charge you with breaking a window all these years later."

Daphne chewed at the inside of her lip. Jessie wasn't sure what had prompted the fib other than her instincts believing Amir's recollection of seeing her.

"Off the record?" Daphne asked.

"Off the record."

"I wanted to get my own back. For Kyle to get his own back. I wanted to ruin her stupid play, but I finished my shift at the car factory too late, and we missed it. A brick through her classroom window felt like the next best thing. I didn't see her there."

"You took your son with you to smash a school window?" Jessie heard the judgement in her voice. "Can he confirm that's all you did?"

"No." Daphne reached around Jessie and pushed in the door. "You can't print that; if you do, I'll deny it, new witness, or not. That woman must have seen us after all."

"What woman?"

"Don't know her name," Daphne said with a shrug, nodding for Jessie to move. "We worked together. She was always in the cafeteria on late shifts at the car factory. Only recognised her because she had on the same ugly cardigan she wore every day. She was walking into the school as we were legging it. That all? I have a café to attend to."

"Then I won't take up more of your time," Jessie reached into her pocket and pulled out a ten-pound note. "Keep the change. The food was excellent."

"If you want my advice? Let the past go. If whoever killed her had been caught then, they'd already have served their time, and they'd be out by now. Who cares what happened all those years ago?"

Jessie bit her tongue as Daphne walked back inside. She quickly typed out as much of what she could remember on her walk back to the bus stop, where Johnny was waiting for her.

"I was beginning to wonder if you'd left without me," he said, relieved. "Did she talk?"

"A little." Jessie tugged off the ID badge and tossed it back. "She called Amir a liar for claiming to have seen her at the school and then admitted to smashing the window in the next breath. And I couldn't get a straight answer about what happened with her son. She had a lot to say, but I still don't know why he was kicked out of school."

"Welcome to the world of journalism." Johnny laughed. "And I can help you there. Kyle was in my class and was a nuisance from the moment he turned up. In all my years in education, he's still the only person I've ever seen bite a teacher. He wasn't the innocent angel she painted in her first interview back in 1989 and he's barely spent a day of his adult life out of prison. They probably have a room with his name on the door. Kyle Nation was a bad egg before Felicity Campbell put her foot down. There's only so much you can do before the bad egg ruins it for everyone else. You caught her in a lie, though? That's impressive. How'd you manage to get her to confess?"

"Lied about a second witness seeing her there. Turned out she saw another woman there, so she didn't question it."

"In the biz, we call that *improvising*." Johnny winked. He pulled out his ticket as the bus rounded the corner. "You know, I think you'd make quite a fine journalist."

As the bus ferried them back to Peridale, Jessie couldn't think about a potential career in journalism. She had Daphne's parting words circling around in her mind.

'Who cares what happened all those years ago?'

Was Daphne trying to warn her to stop digging?

Regardless, Jessie cared, and now that she'd been able to do what her father couldn't and completed the set, she wasn't going to stop.

9

*J*ulia was cheating. She had to be. It felt like she was. She stared at the island where of leaves were drying over every jar, can, and rolling pin that she'd been able to fit on the silver surface. She'd gone into the kitchen for the café's final hour to play with her new toy from the charity shop, but the leaf veiner had turned her into a printing machine. She had plenty of time to clean the café before buffing coloured powders into the microscopic peaks and valleys of the fondant. Fading greens blended into rustic oranges and warm browns. They were so realistic Julia had to stop herself from crumbling one in her hands to check the leaves hadn't transformed themselves into the real things.

Flipping back through the notes she'd made after

her conversation with Libbie, she ticked 'leaves' off her 'wedding cake to-do' list. She still had 'tree bark' and 'moss and vines' to figure out, but at least now she had something to show Leah. Julia tipped her earlier attempts into the bin, happily so.

On her way through the back door, Julia heard Jessie's voice float up from the office. She hadn't even noticed Jessie's return from her Fern Moore trip. She'd been having too much fun playing Mother Nature with sugar and stamps.

Julia took the staircase into the dimly lit office. Barker and Jessie were pacing from different angles while smoky jazz fuzzed from the speakers next to the vinyl player. Julia wondered if it was one of the records she'd picked from the music shop on Mulberry Lane for Barker's recent birthday. She approached to see if the sleeve looked familiar, but the green investigation board diverted her. It was a lot fuller than on her previous visit.

"You've put together a timeline of the day," Julia said, impressed as she scanned the details. "Felicity visited Libbie the day before she went missing trying to get a confession about the stolen money."

"Then that's everyone," Barker said, jotting the detail onto an index card before stabbing it to the board with a pin. "All five of the people accused had contact with Felicity Campbell in the twenty-four hours before she vanished. Walter saw her in the morning, in the staffroom, before she attended the afternoon performance of the play. Then, onto a late lunch in the pub with Molly between three and four, and back to the school around five, crying, as seen by Amir. She was missing by the time the second performance began at seven. At some point after the play, Amir spotted Daphne at the school, and Daphne confessed to smashing Felicity's window."

"Daphne admitted to the window?"

"Jessie squeezed a confession from her," Barker said proudly. "Though I'm not sure what I think about your method. If you did that in the wrong place, impersonating someone from the newspaper could get you in trouble."

"Good thing I did it in the *right* place. Johnny gave me his ID badge, which is as good as permission. And it worked, didn't it? She gave us some new things to investigate. Like this mysterious cardigan-wearing woman she saw at the school."

"Given the way Amir and Daphne have painted that night," Barker said, "the school was quiet enough that Amir thought he was the only witness to Daphne smashing the window. Whoever this woman was, she never came forward. If she was at the school, she might be worth tracking down."

"I wonder if the car factory is still open?" Jessie

asked. "There can't be that many car factories in the area. If it's still around, I could call and ask."

"Ask if they remember a woman from 1989 who wore cardigans?" Barker shook his head. "That'll take you nowhere."

"Well, what do you suggest?"

Barker stopped pacing and joined Julia in taking in the board. Julia skimmed over the notes again. The cardigan note hadn't been written down, but she knew who it could be.

"Molly wears cardigans," Julia thought aloud. "And she mentioned working part-time in a factory when she wasn't in teacher training. She never specified, but it could have been a car factory."

"Then we need to talk to her again," Barker stated. "Did she mention anything about seeing her mother after their lunch?"

"She said that was the last time she saw her."

"Do you think she's lying?" Jessie stood on Julia's other side so all three of them were in a row. "Wasn't she a teacher at the school?"

"Not when I was there," Julia said. The mention of Molly working at the school reminded her of Sue's comment that morning about her being a good teacher. She checked her watch, not wanting to leave it too late to pick up Olivia. Looking back at the board, her eyes landed on the spot between Molly's lunch and Amir's sighting. "If she was last seen at five and the play was at seven, there's a good chance she died in those two hours, but I'm more interested in what happened between four and five to send her back to the school in tears."

"Any of them could have caused that," Barker said. "They were all hostile toward Felicity at some point, and she only seemed to be on positive speaking terms with her daughter near the end."

"Forget Molly," Jessie said quickly. "Walter is the one who wanted to sabotage Felicity. He probably stole the money to ruin her chances of becoming head."

"According to Amir," Barker corrected. "Who waved to her despite having been accused of theft himself? We only have his word on his sighting, and he's still the last person we know of to have seen her alive."

"We only have any of their word," Jessie said with a huff. "He was honest about Daphne smashing that window. Then *and* now. More than we can say about Daphne, who seems to think it's hunky dory to teach her eleven-year-old son that a brick through a window is the answer to consequences. Kyle Nation was in your class, wasn't he, Mum? Johnny said he was a biter."

"I never saw that, but his favourite trick was

throwing chairs across the classroom. On the rare occasions he turned up, he was always involved in some incident or another."

"And rather than focusing on herself, Daphne transferred her anger to her kid's teacher." Jessie folded her arms, clearly deep in thought. "Who knows how long they were at the school? They could have done more than smashing a window."

"Something to consider, but I'd still like to talk to Amir myself," Barker said. "You said you thought he was holding back, and there's a rumour going around that he's the prime suspect."

"You can probably thank my gossiping gran for that," Julia said. "And I think Jessie is right. Mr Harkup has some explaining to do. Libbie thinks he framed her for taking the money, and Amir thinks he started a rumour at the school to incriminate Felicity. Two fingers pointing at the same person. What if Felicity figured out it was him?"

"Have you heard from the head*monster*?" Jessie asked.

Barker checked his phone. "Still nothing. I've left five voicemails. I think it's time to pay him a visit."

"No time like the present." Jessie clapped her hands at the stairs. "Mum can direct the way."

"You'll have to go without me. I need to pick up Olivia."

Julia wrote down the address, and Barker and Jessie headed up the stairs on their latest chase. Julia lingered in the basement for a moment and stared at the timeline.

At four, Felicity had left the pub after a few glasses of champagne with her daughter. What had happened during the following hour to cause her tears? Julia couldn't shake the feeling that the answer to the whole case lay inside that hour.

On their drive to Riverswick, Jessie could barely sit still. She couldn't wait to finally talk to Walter. Properly. Directly. He'd danced around the details of the case like the imp Jessie knew he was. Barker might have been happy dancing to avoid accusing his client, but Jessie wasn't in the mood to tango.

They passed the local college, and the desire to charge at Walter with incriminating questions softened. Sugar worked better than salt. But Jessie had had too many teachers like Walter Harkup. Always thought they were right, no matter what. Always clinging to control. Far too easy to hate. She hadn't minded Mr Jackson, the guy who had helped her scrape through to the end of her course with a certificate to show for her only stable year of education. He'd been as old as Harkup, but time had reduced Mr Jackson to an encouraging grandfatherly figure. She'd never told Julia how close she'd been to throwing in the towel. Mr Jackson had always pulled her back. Walter would have been one of the ones to push her closer to the door.

"Johnny thinks I'd make a good journalist," she said, watching as the college shrank in the side mirror. "But you'd need good grades to do something like that, right?"

"You can do most things without formal education."

"Says the guy with the university degree."

"Maybe not *all* things." Barker glanced at her, but she stared ahead. "But a lot of them. The café not doing it for you?"

"I love it." Jessie thought carefully about how to describe the squirming in her middle. "I just don't love it like Mum loves it. She *really* loves it. It's her passion."

"It's okay if it's just a job to you."

"Maybe it is." Jessie shrugged. "I don't know. Doesn't exactly make me spring out of bed in the morning. Not much has since I got back. Before this case, the days were blurring into one."

"Dark autumn nights will do that to you." Barker flicked on the wipers as the rain came at them from the darkness. "Are you thinking of going back out there?"

"Travelling, you mean?" Jessie shook her head. "No, I'm glad to be home, most of the time. Maybe you're right. Dark autumn nights. Need to get one of those sun lamps or something."

Jessie turned to look out the window as the houses in Riverswick started to balloon in size and drift further apart. The silence grew, broken only by Jessie reading directions from her phone. They pulled up in a cul-de-sac, and Barker cranked up the handbrake. With the engine off, they sat in silence as the rain pounded down on the roof.

"If you want to be a journalist, you could be." Barker ducked to meet her eye line.

"Is this one of 'you can be anything you want to be' talks I've seen in films?"

"No, I could see *you* working as a journalist." Barker's serious tone deflected Jessie's attempt at humour. The rain sped up its drumming as the windows fogged. "You're clearly good at extracting information from people. You've seen the world from more perspectives than most people get the chance to, and if you think more education would help, the resources are there."

"It's too late for all that."

"Jessie, you're twenty." Barker chuckled in a way

that made her feel silly. "I still had years of university ahead of me at your age. I think you'd do well in education for the same reasons you'd make a good journalist. You're inquisitive, curious, and confident."

"But I always found school too difficult."

"You always had a lot of things going on," he said softly. "You're settled now. Don't let the fear of it being difficult hold you back. You couldn't bake a thing before you met Julia, but the café has proved you have the aptitude for learning new skills. If you want to leave—"

"I never said I wanted to leave," Jessie interrupted. "And I don't know if I want to be a journalist. That's half the problem. I don't know *what* I want to do. You're supposed to figure that stuff out at school."

"I don't know many who did." Barker unclipped his seatbelt. "And most of us are still trying to figure out what we want to do. One day you might be forty-two, sitting outside a stranger's office, wondering how it's your job to take pictures of him for his suspicious wife. If twenty is too late to go and find out what you don't know, then I must stand no hope. Sounds to me like you have some unfinished business."

Unfinished business.

Was that it?

Jessie unclipped her seatbelt.

"We have unfinished business here," Jessie said,

redirecting the conversation. "The lights are on, and Walter seems like the sort of person who'd curtain-twitch, so he probably already knows we're here."

Hands cupped at Leah's window, Julia squinted through the gap in the curtains. All the lights were on. With Olivia hugged tight to her against the rain, Julia gave the door a final knock. Still no answer, so she hurried across the lane to her cottage.

"Rox?" Julia called as she kicked off her shoes in the radiator-warmed hallway. "Did you manage to find Leah? Her car is outside her cottage, but she doesn't seem to be—"

Julia passed her sitting room and doubled back. Like on Bonfire Night, Leah was crying in the armchair by the fire, though the tears were more intense, and Johnny wasn't there to snuggle her. After setting Olivia down on the sofa, Julia shrugged off her handbag, hoping her friend's tears were caused by something that Julia could fix with a flash of photorealistic leaves. Surely, she wasn't still this upset about Miss Campbell?

"Leah?" Julia asked softly as she approached with the tissue box. "What is it?"

Leah spluttered through her tears, and no words

came out. Roxy rounded the corner from the kitchen with a steaming mug in her hands. She set tea on the side table next to Leah and perched on the chair arm. Leah folded into her like a ragdoll.

"It's the venue," Roxy said quietly, patting Leah's hair. "They've cancelled."

"*Cancelled*?" Julia shook her head. "This close? How can they have done that?"

"Because they double-booked," Leah punched the words out, anger staining her sobs. "I went to the hotel to give my final payment this morning, and they realised their mistake. The other couple finished paying off months ago. It's over, Julia. The wedding's off."

"The blinds are all down." Jessie's Docs splashed through the puddles as she ran around the side of Walter Harkup's house. "But every room has a light on. I'd say he's hiding. Bang harder."

Barker gave the door another knock. "Any harder, and I'm going to break it down. Maybe he's gone out?"

"And left all the lights on?" Jessie pounded her clenched fist sideways against the wood. "C'mon, Walter, open up. You paid for this. No use hiding now."

Barker gave Jessie an uneasy look before looking around the cul-de-sac as curtains twitched around them. Neighbours' noses peeked out around the circle of identical golden stone cottages. Jessie knew her next bang would likely resort to someone calling the police.

"If he wasn't going to come to the door for that, he wasn't going to come for—"

"Can I help you?"

Jessie and Barker spun to face a polite-looking woman clutching a casserole dish. She wore a chunky knitted brown cardigan, which reminded Jessie why Julia had known where Walter lived.

"Molly Harkup?" Barker got there before Jessie could. "My name is Barker Brown. I'm the PI your father hired to investigate the time capsule case. Do you know his current whereabouts? I'm very eager to talk to him."

"We both are," Jessie cut in.

"At this time, usually at home." Molly lifted the casserole. Carrots swirled around in an unappetising watery beef concoction. "I've been bringing him his food. He hasn't been looking after himself since my mother was found. He's not answering the door, you say?"

"Maybe he'll do it for you?" Barker suggested, stepping to the side. Jessie did the same, and Molly walked between them. "While you're here, we have some questions for you."

"Dad?" Molly's knuckles knocked out a pleasant tune against the frosted glass in the front door. "And I'd be happy to answer any questions you have, Mr Brown. Have you come to give my father updates about the case?"

"I'm here because I can't get in touch with him," Barker said as Molly crouched to poke up the letterbox in the middle of the door. "When did you last see your father?"

"Last night around this same time," she said, peering through the narrow view into the hallway. "Pasta bake yesterday. His favourite. *Dad*? It's Molly. Are you in?"

Barker tried his best to match Molly's awkwardly gracious smile while they waited for an answer huddled under the small roof above the door. Around them, the curtains continued to move. One woman, who had a garden full of gnomes, was on the phone as she peered around the edge of the curtain. Jessie couldn't imagine much happened here if their visit was causing such a stir.

"Do you have a key?" Barker asked.

"Sorry, no." Molly offered an apologetic smile. "I always said I should have one for emergencies, but there comes an age where people get terribly stuck in their ways. My father used to have a study at home to which only he had a key. I was only allowed in there if I'd done something particularly exceptional or something naughty. He's a man who enjoys his privacy."

"Sounds to me like he takes his work home with him," Jessie muttered, almost to herself. "A garden with that many intact gnomes, you mustn't have a lot of crime around here. I'd feel safe leaving a key somewhere outside. Maybe he told you about one?"

"Oh, erm." Molly thought for a moment. "Yes, now that you mention it, I think he keeps a key under the back doormat."

Jessie was the first to reach the back of the house. She ripped back the doormat, and there was no key. A golden patch of the flagstone shone up in the shape of a key among moss like a missing jigsaw piece.

"Looks like it was recently taken," Jessie said.

"He has been rather paranoid lately. He might have removed it." Molly placed the casserole dish on the patio table. She walked over to the back door. "Didn't my father come to your office for a meeting?"

"No?"

"That's what he told me when I brought the pasta bake. He said he'd found out something that he thought would help with your investigation." Molly knocked at the back door's frosted glass and listened. "He seemed rather excited about it."

"Did he say what it was?"

Molly shook her head. "No. He seemed to be in a hurry to get rid of me. At first, I thought he was tired after an afternoon of being interrogated by the police, but he kept checking his watch."

"Like he was waiting for someone?"

"Perhaps?" Molly stepped back from the door and returned to her casserole. "He doesn't seem to be in."

Jessie peered at the upstairs windows. All the lights were on, and unlike the kitchen, the blinds were rolled up. She walked back down the long garden on her tiptoes, and more of the rooms came into view. She could see Walter's bedroom, where the bed was neatly made, and into a study. Unless he was ducking under the windows, both rooms appeared to be empty. Jessie looked back to the house with a sigh. Molly clutched her casserole, and Barker had his phone at his ear. Looking to the kitchen's back door, Jessie waited for the sound of a phone. None came, but something caught her eye through the frosted glass panels.

Something red.

Jessie ran backwards down the garden and squinted until the red blur turned into a shape. A headless shape, but the form of a person all the same.

Before Barker or Molly could say anything to stop her, Jessie picked up a rock from the garden and smashed it through the obscured glass.

"What on earth are you doing?" Molly cried. "You've broken the window!"

"*Jessie*?" Barker ran at her as her hand scrambled for the handle on the other side. "What do you think you're..."

Barker didn't finish his sentence as the door pushed inwards, revealing what had come into focus on Jessie's backwards jog down the garden. In his red cardigan, Walter Harkup was slumped at the kitchen table with his face in a plate of pasta bake, though that was the least of his worries. The black handle of a kitchen knife jutted from between his shoulder blades. Barker checked his pulse, but Jessie knew there wasn't much point. Walter hadn't had the rosiest cheeks, but they hadn't been as grey as dust.

"What's going on?" Molly called as she approached the back door. "Have you found—" She screamed and let go of the casserole dish. It smashed, sending chunks of beef and carrot slices skidding across the wet flagstones in all directions. "Dad? Is he..."

"I'm sorry, Molly," Barker said, stepping back and crunching something under his shoe. Sounded like dry pasta. "He's dead. We need to get out of here."

"Dad?" Molly rushed over to him and shook his shoulder. "Oh, Dad. Not like this."

"It's a crime scene, Molly." Barker lifted his shoe. It wasn't pasta. Looked more like wood. "We've already disturbed it enough."

Barker guided Molly back into the rain, but Jessie couldn't pull herself away. She crouched to look at the pieces of wood. More were scattered around the tiles – intact tiny wooden balls. Jessie pulled out her phone and snapped a picture. Barker called for her, and she left, but not without taking a last look at Walter.

They never would get to talk to him.

Jessie had been so sure he'd been up to something, but going off Molly's account, Walter had figured things out without them and died because of it.

The secret couldn't die with him.

Jessie wouldn't let it.

10

---

*D*espite the continuing rain, the café was packed to capacity fifteen minutes before noon the following day. Murder would do that. Dot was leading the public conversation, never more in her element than when she had an audience. Murder would do that too. Holding court kept Dot so busy Julia hadn't even needed to dodge any conversations about a reunion of their defunct neighbourhood watch lately. At least one good thing had come from the recent chaos.

And that had to be the only good thing. Tray first, Julia brushed through the beads and into the kitchen. Johnny still looked as crushed as when he'd sat down. Julia set the lattes on the island before serving slices of the pumpkin spice fruit cake.

"Your wedding cake," Julia said, offering him a fork. "The inside, at least."

"Roxy was just showing me your leaves. They're incredible." Johnny struggled to produce a smile before he took a bite. "Absolutely delicious. But I hate to say it – I don't think there's going to be a wedding. The time capsule dampened the whole thing, and now Walter too. Leah's completely given up, and I don't know what to do."

"We're not going to let her give up," Roxy said firmly. "We won't let her, will we, Julia?"

"There has to be a fix." Julia carried over her morning's attempt at creating bark out of icing. "Only a trial, but I haven't given up. There must be some way we can sort this out. Another venue?"

"Leah had her heart set on this hotel." Johnny pushed a piece of dried fruit around the plate with the fork prongs. "She's been putting little pins in things all the years she's been wedding planning. All the best places, the best venues, best dressmakers, the best florists, the best caterers." He took another bite. "The best baker, too. Every wedding, she offers brides the best of the best and then they have the final say. This was her chance to do everything exactly how she wanted."

"Again," Roxy added. "Are we just going to pretend she hasn't been married a few times before?"

"Well, this is the *first* time it's true love." Julia gave Roxy a stern look. "But Roxy's right about not letting her give up. We can't let her. "

"I'm not sure if there's any convincing her," Johnny said, downtrodden. "I tried all last night and this morning. What if this isn't about the venue? What if she ... she doesn't want to marry me?"

"Don't be a wally, Johnny." Roxy whacked his arm with the back of her hand. "We all know what Leah is like. She was always the teacher's pet. She gives one hundred and ten percent to everything, and she's put this venue on a pedestal. Nothing else will compare in her mind, but she'll almost probably snap out of it." She paused to sip her latte. "Last time I checked, a wedding was about two people coming together in love. She's just letting her meticulousness get in the way. We just need to make her realise so we can get this show back on the road. We still have two weeks to figure something out."

"One week and four days." Johnny took a big bite of the cake and, through the mouthful, said, "There is another reason she wants things to be perfect."

Julia and Roxy exchanged glances as he chewed.

"Spit it out, Johnny," Roxy said.

"The cake?"

"No, the other reason," Julia said. "You sounded serious."

"And then took a dramatic pause."

"Because I'm not sure if I should say," he whispered, looking toward the curtain into the café. "I promised Leah I wouldn't, but—"

"She's *pregnant*!" Roxy cut in. "I *knew* it. Didn't I say, Julia? Explains all the crying."

"No," Johnny said with a frown. "Leah's just in touch with her emotions. You should try it sometime."

"Never have time." Roxy wafted her hand. "If not that, then what is it?"

"It's not about Leah. It's about me." He fiddled with his glasses as his pale cheeks flushed scarlet. "But it does affect both of us. We weren't going to say anything until after the wedding. We haven't fully decided yet, but it's something we've talked about and…"

In the silence, Julia heard what he was struggling to say. "You're moving away."

"Maybe?" Johnny said, clenching one eye. "Maybe not? As I said, we haven't decided, but we've been discussing it. I've been offered a new job."

Julia couldn't help but look at Roxy, who had started silently eating the cake. Roxy still didn't know that Julia had seen the Liverpool school application form on her laptop. She'd almost brought it up in Richie's, but hadn't wanted reality to ruin their bubble of fun. Julia's mouth was suddenly dry.

"A job?" Julia pushed through a smile for Johnny. "That's fantastic news. What for, and where?"

"A media firm in Manchester," he said with an almost apologetic smile. "Makes the people I work for look like amateurs. That's part of the reason they want me. They heard how much I was doing at *The Peridale Post* with little support from the higher-ups. They've been cutting back and choking me for years. Constantly having to rescue a dying paper propped up in a small Cotswold village wasn't exactly where I thought my journalism career would go. They've offered me a *real* opportunity. I'd be heading a whole team of people, and the money ... the money is great. Really great. It's a chance to progress that I'll never get here."

"That sounds perfect, Johnny," Julia said after giving him a hug. "I'm so proud of you."

"It sounds amazing, mate." Roxy couldn't seem to bring herself to look at Johnny – or Julia, for that matter.

"Like I said, we haven't decided," Johnny said quickly. "Since I was headhunted, they've given me until after Christmas to decide. It's a strange feeling to have someone appreciate what I can do. They seem excited to work with me."

"This could be the end of an era," Julia said, and she found herself sniffing back tears. "This wedding must go ahead. Leah wants it to go ahead. She just needs reminding."

"What do you suggest?" Johnny asked. "And keep this between us. Leah included. I promised we'd tell you together if we decided. I wasn't sure how you'd take it. You've barely said anything, Rox."

"I'm happy for you." Roxy slipped out of her chair and gave Johnny a reluctant-looking hug. "Like Julia said, end of an era. Everything changes eventually. It's not like we've all lived here the whole time. We're all big enough to know that's how the world works. Julia? Say something to lift the mood because I'm not very good at this part. What do we do?"

"We save the wedding," Julia said, tilting her head at her latest experiment. "I've put too much time into this cake, and I'm determined to see it cut. Call every venue in the area and compile a list of those available for next Saturday. That might be enough to shake Leah into action."

"Not a bad idea," Johnny said, sliding his laptop from his messenger bag. "Leah does love a list. Roxy, get your phone out. I'll search, you call."

Leaving her friends to start sorting out the wedding mess, Julia returned to the café. She busied herself with wiping down the coffee machine. She wasn't sure how she felt about Johnny's confession. They'd all spent their time away from the village in adulthood. These last few years since Leah's return had been the first time they'd all been in their home village since their teen years. Julia hadn't considered how long it would last, but she wasn't sure how to face the idea of losing her three closest friends in one swoop.

"You good?" Jessie whispered. "You're polishing the same spot."

Nothing was set in stone.

They still had the wedding to get through.

To savour their time together.

"I was miles away."

Julia tossed down the rag and looked out to the café. Every seat was filled, but there was a restless energy in the air, and Dot was helping whip up a good deal of it. She was in the middle of the café, arms folded, foot tapping, eyes on the clock.

"What are you waiting for, Gran?"

"*Who* we're all waiting for," Dot corrected, motioning to the café. "Why else do you think I gathered everyone here today? You said DI Moyes was coming for a community meeting this afternoon."

"That's not quite what I said."

"You said she was open. First Felicity Campbell and *now* the headteacher."

"And after last night, she will likely be swamped today."

"Then let's hope she squeezes us in. We deserve to know what is going on with this investigation. It's a shambles, a disgrace, a catastrophe!"

A rumble of agreement reverberated around the café.

"And she's late," Dot grumbled. "She said afternoon. It's *after* noon."

Julia glanced at the clock.

Five minutes past twelve.

It was going to be a long day.

The collective waiting – only interrupted by Dot functioning as a speaking clock to a backdrop of pattering rain – started to drive Jessie so mad she found herself lounging on faraway beaches. She blamed Alfie's latest picture for the daydreaming. He was somewhere called Hot Water Beach in New Zealand, where the water lived up to its name thanks to a volcano heating it to the point of steam. Jessie was still disappointed she hadn't seen turtles at Turtle Beach in Turkey.

The arrival of Molly Harkup pulled Jessie back to dreary, chilly Peridale. Molly hurried through the door in a knitted scarf that looked like it had been made entirely from scraps. By the lack of pouncing,

Dot didn't recognise her. Jessie wouldn't have known her if she hadn't seen her the previous night. She'd barely been able to sleep, Molly's scream and smashing casserole dish playing on a loop in her mind like a rabid Tik Tok video she couldn't scroll past.

"*Molly?*" Dot announced after someone whispered to her. "We're all terribly sorry about what happened to your father. Quite shocking. How are you doing?"

"I've been better," Molly said with a sigh. "But thank you for asking. That's really kind of you. I'm not sure we've met?"

"I'm the grandmother of your father's former private investigator's wife," Dot said earnestly. "My thoughts are with you. We're all very concerned about what's going on." She paused, scratching at the back of her short curls. "I don't suppose the police have told you what's going on?"

"I'm afraid not," she said, bowing herself away from Dot and toward the counter. "But the private investigator is why I'm here. Julia, my father said your husband's office was downstairs. I couldn't find the door."

"This way," Jessie said, jumping up.

Barker kicked his feet off the desk and brushed away crumbs. He'd snuck up to grab a slice of chocolate cake an hour ago. Olivia babbled at Molly from the floor, her hands reaching for the trailing scarf as Molly walked past. Molly fluffed it at Olivia's face.

"Molly," Barker rose to his feet, licking chocolate from his lips as he held out his hand. "How are you feeling?"

"As you'd expect," she said with a little less vigour than the public civility she'd put on upstairs. Jessie didn't doubt Dot was flat to the floorboards. "I could barely sleep last night, and as tired as I am, I can't stand the thought of sitting around doing nothing. It's what the police want me to do. I hope you don't mind me coming here unannounced. I was in the village to speak with the cold case team, and I wanted to come and see you as soon as possible."

"Not at all," Barker said, pulling up his chair and nodding at the record player. Jessie hurried in to turn it down to his 'client level'. "Did they have anything to tell you?"

"Only that my father was likely stabbed Sunday night somewhere between seven and ten. They can't be any more accurate given how long he was there," she said. "It looks like someone used the key under the doormat to let themselves in to stab him while he ate his dinner. I was across the road the whole time."

"You mustn't blame yourself," Barker said.

"I could have spared you both having to see that if

only I'd gone over earlier," she said, sniffing back tears and plucking a tissue from the box on the counter. "Seeing the bodies of both of my parents in one week is certainly an experience I'll never forget and one I'm glad I'll never repeat. I know some people aren't so lucky to get to my age with both of their parents still alive, but I really did think my dad had more left in the tank. He was to retire this year. He collected trains. Has since I was little." She smiled down into her lap, her lips trembling as the tears dropped into her clutched tissue. "He was finally going to build a track in his attic. He dreamed of creating his own little town and painting all the buildings. I can't believe he's gone." She cleared her throat. "I can't sit around and do nothing. It's not in my character. If you're free to do so, I wish to employ you to pick up where my father left off. I imagine the same person committed both murders, so it goes without saying that I want my father's death to be included in your investigation. Will you take the case?"

Jessie couldn't believe Barker's hesitation. He hadn't jumped at the chance to take the case from Walter the first time around either, but now he looked like he might turn Molly down as he wrung his hands.

"Of course we'll take the case," Jessie answered for him. "We're not going to stop until we know what happened. Are we, Dad?"

"No," he said, leaning against the desk, clamping his fingers together. "The case continues."

"Thank you," Molly said, fumbling in her pockets and producing a small purse. "I don't have much in savings, but if you take credit cards, that'll be—"

"No charge, Miss Harkup." Barker held up a hand. "Your father paid more than enough for the investigation to continue for a while. Don't worry about it."

"Really, thank you." Molly lowered her head and dabbed her eyes. "I have every faith in you. Do you have any updates about how the case is going?"

"We have some questions," Jessie said, glancing at the timeline. "A woman fitting your description was seen at St. Peter's sometime after the play, when your mum's classroom window was smashed."

"Are you suggesting that I smashed a window?"

"No, we know who did that," Jessie said. "But you don't deny being at the school? When my mum asked, you said the last time you saw your mum was at the pub over lunch."

"Yes, it was," Molly said with a firm nod. "And yes, I did go to the school. I didn't mention that because she asked when I last *saw* her. I didn't see my mum at the school. I went to see how the play had gone, but I couldn't find her. The police turned up to deal with whatever happened with the window. They asked if I'd seen anything, which I hadn't, so they let me go home. Why is it important?"

"Just a follow-up," Barker said. "But while we're asking questions, I've been eager to ask how your mother seemed during lunch that day? Julia said you'd spent years going over that day trying to find some hint that she was planning to run to Scotland. Now that you know the truth, have you gone over the day again? What kind of spirits was she in?"

"High spirits," Molly said. "She was excited about the play. It was always her favourite time of year."

"And she gave no indication she'd found out something new about the stolen money?"

"None at all." Molly looked between them. "Has something new been uncovered? Did she find out the truth before she died?"

"There's an unaccounted-for hour," Barker said.

"Between four and five," Jessie said, tapping the gap in their timeline. She'd already added 'Molly' to the 'cardigan woman' note. "She left you in high spirits at four, and she was seen sobbing by five. Any idea what could have happened?"

"Like I said, I never saw her again after we parted at the pub. What do you suppose happened during that hour?"

"Best not to speculate," Barker said with a tight

smile. "It's a thread for us to pull on, though. Is there anything else you think we should know?"

Molly thought for a moment before standing.

"Nothing I can think of, Mr Brown, but I'm afraid I've passed beyond the point of tired now, and I need to sleep." Molly tossed her scarf around herself, smiling at Olivia as she once again marvelled at the tassels. Molly's smile soured. "Do I need to be worried, Mr Brown?"

"About what?"

"Both of my parents have been murdered," Molly said stiffly. "Do you think there's a chance that I'm next?"

When Detective Inspector Laura Moyes entered the café at almost three, the waiting crowd were hungry for blood. They offered a sarcastic round of applause like a medieval crowd welcoming the executioner who'd been hiding too long at the local pub.

"About time!" Dot announced after the applause petered out. "Out making arrests, I hope?"

DI Moyes arched a brow across the rowdy café to Julia. She offered an apologetic smile, but there wasn't much she could do for the DI now. The people had questions, and Julia feared a riot if the DI didn't throw them something to devour.

"We're following many promising lines of inquiry," DI Moyes said, her husky voice struggling to project around the room.

"That's police talk for 'we have no idea what's going on', isn't it?" Dot said. "You can't fool us. What's going on? Two people are dead, thirty years apart. There's a killer at large. We want to know what you're doing about it."

"Sifting through evidence and interviews from thirty years ago isn't an easy task, I can assure you," DI Moyes said, glancing up at the ceiling with a sigh. "You want information? So far, we know that Felicity Campbell was likely murdered on November 24th, the last day she was seen in Peridale."

"We know that already," Dot said.

"She was poisoned." Moyes' words cut through the growing rumbling. "Some information we only confirmed this morning after many lengthy and expensive forensic tests were carried out."

"Poisoned?" Evelyn gasped. "Oh my, that's horrible."

"Poisoned by what?" Julia asked.

"Methanol," Moyes replied. "The simplest form of alcohol. It has many uses, is used in many industries, and is incredibly toxic to humans when ingested. One hundred millilitres of the stuff are enough to kill a person without the proper medical attention, which Felicity did not get. What else?" Moyes stared off into nothingness as she searched her mind. "We confirmed that the letters are forgeries after a new analysis."

"How did that slip through the first time?" someone asked.

"An ancient, incompetent handwriting specialist months from retirement," Moyes said, holding up both hands. "Which, believe me, is as frustrating to me as it is to you. Felicity would still have died, and we might never have found her if not for the recent digging at the school, but the investigation shouldn't have been closed in 1990. On behalf of the police, I'm sorry this happened. Does anyone know anything else that can help with this case?"

"What about the groundskeeper?" someone asked. "I heard he did it."

"I'm not here to speculate about rumours. A word, Julia?"

DI Moyes crossed the café as a flurry of questions leapt up. She walked around the counter and through the beads. Julia followed her through. Roxy and Johnny looked up, but DI Moyes didn't show interest in what they were doing.

"What was that about?" Moyes demanded. "I thought we would have a quiet chat and share ideas?"

"My gran got carried away, as my gran tends to, but it comes from a good place, I assure you. She wants to know what's going on. As do I."

"And me," Johnny said.

"Me too," Roxy added. "Walter was my boss. Felicity was my teacher."

"And I assure you, we are doing everything we can," DI Moyes said, her gaze lingering on Roxy, "but what was found last night complicates things. This isn't just a cold case anymore. Julia, I came here to get your opinion of Liberty Turner. Libbie. You spoke with her before I did, and yet I couldn't get much. Did she say anything to you?"

"She told me her parents sent her down from Scotland to live with Felicity. She also told me about stealing from them but turning things around. She denied taking the charity money." Julia thought for a moment. "She didn't like Walter. She claimed he framed her, and when she talked about the divorce, she mentioned that she thought Felicity was better off with someone else. When I pushed her about whom, she wouldn't say."

"A secret lover?" Moyes seemed taken aback by the news. "That could be something to explore, thank you. If you don't know anything else, I need to go. You *must* cease your investigation immediately, Julia."

The directness of her words took Julia by surprise.

"What happened to being open to working with the community?"

"That was before a man was murdered in the present day." Moyes gave a patronising smile as though it should have been obvious. "You'll understand it's best not to throw yourself into trouble when you don't need to. Besides, it looks like you have your hands full with this place. It must be quite the little earner. Quite adorable."

DI Moyes nodded to each of them and exited through the back.

"I still can't tell if she's being sincere or sarcastic when she gives those little compliments."

"I'm glad you said it. Again," Roxy said. "Are you going to listen to her and stay out?"

"What do you think?"

11

Once the café was closed for the day, Jessie returned to Fern Moore by car. Barker pulled up in the small car park, his headlights shining ahead at a gang who looked too old to hang around a children's play area. Daphne's was open, and just like the night before, it was the centre of the buzz.

"Don't go into police mode on her," Jessie said as they crossed the courtyard in the rain. "If we're going to find out where everyone was the night Walter died, we have to be cool about it."

"I'll be on my best behaviour. If you're still pretending you're from the paper, don't you think it'll look odd that we're here together?"

"Let's see what happens."

They didn't have to wait long. Daphne abandoned scooping baked beans on a plate and marched to meet them on the other side of the counter. Her seeping anger silenced the café.

"I told you to stop coming here," she cried at Barker, pointing at the door. "*Out*! You're not wanted. I don't care if you're *former* police. You're all the same to me. You put Carol's nephew away." Daphne cast a finger at a glaring woman. "And Jeff's grandson."

"She's told you to clear off twice before," Jeff, the old man who'd wanted the ketchup, called from behind. Jessie wondered if Jeff was Daphne's Dot. Always around, always paying attention. "Do as you're told and run back to the village."

"And *you've* got some nerve." Daphne looked Jessie up and down with a venomous glare, her hands planted on her hips. "I called the paper. There's no article about me being printed. You're not a journalist at all, are you?"

"I'm not," Jessie admitted. The stares of the full café burned into her, and she appreciated the draft from the nearby the door. "But I knew you'd never talk to me if I told you my dad was the PI looking into the Felicity Campbell case."

"You're right. I wouldn't have." Daphne's eyes darted between them, and she worked something around in her mouth. "I should have known. You look alike. Spitting image."

Jessie and Barker glanced at each other; neither jumped in to let her know that was impossible. Daphne could keep the wrong end of this stick. Her shoulders lost their hunch, though her eyes stared all the same.

"You will have heard about Walter?" Jessie asked.

"Stabbed in the back, I heard." Daphne cleared her throat. "Good riddance to the lot of them. They all failed my son."

"We're not here to talk about that," Jessie said, moving closer to the counter with cautious steps. "We want to know where you were Sunday night between seven and ten."

Daphne's eyes narrowed. "Are you accusing me?"

"The police will ask the same question, if they haven't already," Barker said. "If you've got nothing to hide..."

Barker left the question hanging. Maybe a sprinkle of police wasn't a bad thing. The leading question was making Daphne consider her options.

"I was at Platts Social Club all night on Sunday." Daphne folded her arms tightly. "Karaoke night."

"I saw her there," Jeff called out.

"Yeah, me too."

"Same."

"We all did."

Daphne looked pleased with herself.

"What did you sing?" Barker asked.

"'Total Eclipse of the Heart'," Daphne answered, deadpan. "Bonnie Tyler. Jeff did the backing vocals."

"'*Turn around, bright eyes*'," Jeff sang. "We were quite the duo."

"If that's all you came for, clear off," Daphne called. "I'm not answering any more of *your* questions, and you're not welcome to eat here. Neither of you."

The door opened, and Jessie stepped out of the way to let in the newcomer. She turned to see the gang from the park crowded around the door. The burliest of the bunch leaned into the café, looking Barker up and down.

"Trouble, Daph?"

"These two were just leaving," she said, her grin growing. "Close the door on your way. You're letting all the heat out."

Jessie and Barker exchanged glances before setting off to the door. The gang barely parted around them, leaving them to fight through a cloud of aftershave and beer fumes. A can trailed after them as they walked to the car, but Barker didn't stop.

"Platts is just around the corner," he said, taking

jogs between every few footsteps. "Was always a den of trouble. Spent far too many of my weekends here, trying to figure out who threw the first punch."

Jessie glanced over her shoulder. The gang were following. She sped up as Barker turned the corner around the back of the block of flats. Platts Social Club stood alone behind a small car park. Christmas lights switched between red and green around its sign. They approached the front door, with the gang lingering on the pavement under a lamppost.

"Karaoke, eight till midnight every Sunday." Barker tapped a poster encased in plastic. "We could go in and ask, but I know how that goes. Just mentioning Daphne's name will have them confirm any alibi."

"Didn't you believe her?"

"People protect their own around here."

"You don't know what it's like to live in places like this," she said, glancing back at the gang, who were doing nothing but watching. "People turning up in fancy cars wearing suits and asking questions rarely ends well. I think it might be time to get back to the car if we're not going inside. We're being followed, and I'd rather they not follow us somewhere we don't know the exits."

"Let's take her at her word and rule her out for

now," Barker said, pulling out his car keys. "Now, time for a police officer's approach."

Julia flicked through her notepad using the spotlights under her cabinets as a reading light. After Molly's meeting with Barker, she couldn't stop herself from going over all the details again. She'd hoped to draw some concrete conclusions from her reams and reams of notes, but she only saw holes.

The methanol.

The knife.

The time capsule.

Julia wasn't sure how any of it fit together.

Like Jessie, Julia had started leaning toward Mr Harkup because of the theory he'd stolen the money. Now that the headteacher was dead, Julia's only conclusion was that she wanted to talk to the two people who had questioned his innocence in the first place – Libbie and Amir.

"I only sent you in here to get the matches." Roxy popped her head around the doorframe, tilting back so her sheet mask didn't slide off. "Have a night off, Julia. Now that Walter's dead, the police will surely figure it out. Like Moyes said earlier, it's not a cold case anymore. Are they called hot cases when they're not cold?" Roxy leaned in and swiped the box of matches off the corner of the breakfast bar. "Can't be a spa without candles. Whatever's in the cake box smells good."

Julia smiled. "Have a look."

Roxy flipped the lid. "Cinnamon rolls!"

"I made them especially."

"I'll never know if Harkup did steal my cinnamon roll now," she said drily, closing the lid and stacking it under the matches. "Not unless he left a confession made out of pasta shapes?"

"No such luck."

Roxy left the kitchen. Julia pulled herself away, shaking the paper free of the flaked-off crumbs of her clay face mask. It wasn't like she would leave the cottage until tomorrow. She glanced into Olivia's bedroom on her way to the sitting room. Soundly asleep.

"I don't know what any of this stuff does," Roxy said, lifting a glass wand attached to a plastic handle. She twisted a dial, and the glass fizzed with a red glow. "I'm not sure I want to know."

"High-frequency wand," Leah said. "You run it over your face and it kills bacteria."

Roxy touched it to her face and winced. Julia heard a slight sizzle. "It zapped me! And this?" Roxy jammed on a white mask with only a slit for eyes, her face turning different colours as she played with the remote. "I look like that woman on *The Cube* who shows you how to do the challenges. When I said to bring your spa stuff, I thought mud masks and nail files."

"Times have moved on," Leah said, settling further into the armchair, wriggling her toes in front of the snapping fire. "I'd go crazy without my routine. It's my self-care after long, stressful days with bridezillas and pushy mothers. I refuse to let them age me."

Julia had never seen any of the beauty gizmos and gadgets Leah had brought over, and she couldn't imagine how much they cost. Still, Leah did seem to be calming down the more she pushed a jade roller across her neck and jawline. She hadn't cried since they'd started their spa night, which had been Roxy's idea.

"You do look the youngest of us." Roxy tugged off the plastic mask. "Julia, are you okay? You're not saying much."

"Mask," she mumbled through clay so tight she couldn't open her mouth without it cracking. "How long?"

"The Aztec clay?" Leah reached out for the tub and turned it over. "Ten to fifteen minutes."

"Mate, you were in there for ages," Roxy said with

a snort, kicking her feet onto the coffee table. "Half an hour, easily."

Julia went into the bathroom and washed off the mask, which wasn't as easy as she remembered from the masks she'd dabbled with in her teens. The clay had fused to her skin. She scrubbed with a hand cloth until she felt the sweet release. After splashing her face, she stared at herself in the mirror and hoped her face was red from the scrubbing. Dabbing herself off with a towel, Julia left the bathroom. Johnny was in the hallway, pulling off his messenger bag.

"Crikey, Julia." Johnny gasped. "Halloween was last month."

"Leah, will this redness go down?"

"You just need to moisturise," Leah said, squinting at Julia through the dimly lit sitting room. "You do look a bit peachy."

"Moisture!" Roxy called, waving a foil-encased sheet mask above her head. "Come and join me. We can look like the guy from *Texas Chainsaw Massacre* together."

Julia pulled the gooey fabric mask from the packet and picked it apart.

"Having fun?" Johnny asked, perching on Leah's chair arm. "Did you get anywhere calling that list of venues?"

"No luck," Leah said, exhaling – though not

crying. "Of the four numbers you found, two had booked up with corporate Christmas parties in the hours before I called, and the other two said it was too short notice for them to be staffed for a wedding. I think it's a sign we should postpone and circle back in the spring."

"Spring? Don't you want us to get married, Leah?"

"Are you seriously asking me that?" Leah's sheet mask puckered at her brows. Julia finished untangling hers and settled it across her skin, the slimy coldness refreshing her stinging cheeks. "Johnny, this has *everything* to do with our wedding and *nothing* to do with our future marriage. The hotel's next availability is in spring. I've done so much planning. I can't just throw it away now."

"To hell with plans." Johnny's voice rose, and Roxy clutched Julia's arm, no doubt from the shock. If there'd been popcorn, Roxy would have grabbed a handful. "I've come up with a plan. The church and village hall are available. The wedding you planned would be the wedding of the century, no question about it, but we're inviting twenty-five people, Leah. At the end of the evening, when we're dancing around that dance floor as husband and wife, are we going to care about any of the details?"

Johnny dropped down to one knee, and Roxy's fingers dug into Julia's flesh. Julia tilted her head back as the eyeholes of her sheet mask slipped down.

"Leah, will you marry me this Saturday at St. Peter's Church, with a reception at the village hall next door?" Johnny asked, taking both her hands in his. "I know it's not the glamorous venue you wanted, but it's right here in our home, a stone's throw from the school where we first met when we were four years old."

"Did you say *this* Saturday?" Roxy interjected.

"Things really are booked up around here this time of year," Johnny said. "What do you say, Leah?"

"Oh, Johnny, this might be the second most romantic thing you've done after your actual proposal," Leah said, biting her lip. "But there's just *so* much to do. Half the reason I picked that venue was that it was an all-inclusive service. Food, décor, they supply it all. All those meetings, all those decisions..." She clenched her eyes shut. "Would we be able to? It's in *four* days. We'd need to find caterers, decorations, tables..."

"I can put together a dessert buffet," Julia said without hesitation. "And we'll help however we can, won't we, Roxy?"

"Bridesmaids attending to duty." Roxy saluted. "Though the school is reopening tomorrow. Not looking forward to the remembrance assembly they've planned. Kids are going to be distraught. I could get them to make some paperchains during their art lesson. Something easy, and we can hang them up at the village hall."

"And I gave a glowing review to the sandwich shop on Mulberry Lane, and they do buffets," Johnny said, still on one knee. "We can do this, Leah. You know we can. We can figure it out together. I'd marry you at a motorway service station if I had to."

Leah peeled off her mask and gave Johnny a kiss.

"This is bonkers," she said. "I guess I need to send out some new invitations. I'm getting married this Saturday."

"Wait?" Roxy sat forward, and her mask gave up and slid off. "Does that mean this is the hen party? Johnny, get to the shop. We need champagne."

Jessie handed a maple and cinnamon hot chocolate to a gloved forensic officer. They'd handed out almost all of the sixteen cups they'd driven over from the café in cardboard trays. She was surprised at how well Barker's plan had worked.

"You've caused an unauthorised strike at my crime scene," Detective Inspector Moyes said as she strode through Walter's front door. Behind, Jessie could see right down the hall to the kitchen. She could still see the image of Walter facedown in the pasta. "Who told you to do this?"

"Nobody," Barker said, handing her a hot chocolate. She clutched it and stared like she had no idea what to do with it. "But I know what long nights on a cold, wet crime scene are like. I thought you could all do with something warm to pick you up."

DI Moyes frowned at Barker, but she took a sip. She enjoyed it, Jessie could tell from the squint of her eyes, but she seemed to have mastered every muscle in her face to not show much else.

"Barker Brown, I take it. What do you want?"

"Take a break." Barker put the final hot chocolate tray on the doorstep, and another two people in white suits wriggled them out. "There's cake in the car. Detective Inspector-only perk."

Barker set off as though he knew DI Moyes would follow, which she did. Jessie climbed into the back seat, leaving Moyes to sit in the front. She fingered open the paper bag on the dashboard.

"Fruit cake?" she said with a groan. "You'd have been better going with something with cream. Or make an appointment through the station."

"I thought we could talk DI to PI," he said, opening his hands. "We're both working toward the same goal. We want to know what happened. The only differences are access and employer."

DI Moyes glanced toward Molly's cottage as she plucked the fruit cake from the bag. She took a bite.

"Your wife made this?"

"She did."

"Pretty good." She went for a second bite. "What do you want to know?"

"What's going on?"

"And here I was hoping you'd have some *specific* questions." Jessie saw Moyes' eyes roll in the rear-view mirror. "Honestly, my money was on the ex-husband. It's usually the spouse. Now that he's been stabbed between the shoulder blades, we hope DNA analysis returns with a result. Thank you for contaminating my crime scene, by the way. We've eliminated you both from the data set, don't worry."

"I'm honoured."

"Your alibis checked out."

"We have Daphne at karaoke," Jessie said. "Confirmed it?"

"Enough witnesses came forward," she said. "Amir claims he was at home with his son, which the son confirmed. Molly was at the school painting the set, where she signed the guestbook on arrival and entry, and Libbie said she was babysitting. Can you add to any of that?"

"I'm afraid not, Detective."

"Then why did you drag me away from my work?" She put the rest of the fruit cake in the bag and tossed it back on the dashboard. "You know, I heard you were one of the good ones. Why'd you quit?"

"I'm not sure," Barker said. "Felt like the right thing to do at the time. I liked the sound of being my own boss."

"How's that working out for you?" Moyes took a slurp of the hot chocolate and crammed it into the cup holder. "Thanks for the break, but I need to get back to solving this case."

DI Moyes climbed out of the car and walked around the back. She knocked on Barker's window, making them both jump. He rolled it down, and she leaned in.

"I'll tell you two things," she said in a low voice. "The knife you found in Walter's back isn't the knife that killed him."

"Other means?"

"No, he *was* stabbed," she said, "but the blade that killed him was three inches longer than the one we pulled out, and it had completely different blade markings. What do you make of that?"

"Two people stabbed him, one after the other?" Barker suggested immediately. "Or the knife was swapped?"

"That's where my mind went," she said, stepping back from the car and onto the pavement. "Might not be relevant, but it's something to think about."

"And the second thing?"

"I'm only in the village for the cold case," she said, offering her first smile as she stepped back onto the pavement. "Your successor, Christie, isn't getting his DI job back. They haven't announced it yet, but it's going to happen. They're going to need to fill his role. Just something to think about."

Barker nodded, but he didn't say anything. He rolled up his window, and after they both agreed that the two knives thing was strange, he spent their journey back to Peridale in silence.

Jessie didn't need to ask what he was thinking about.

Julia hadn't intended to leave the cottage again. Still, she couldn't stop herself from going to the café once Barker returned with the news from the crime scene. Leah and Roxy had already left, their hen party cut short after a few glasses of champagne so Leah could get started with the new plans. Julia jotted down Barker's notes, but with only four days until the wedding, she had to choose the cake over the case.

Working in her bright kitchen as the wind whipped at the lashing rain outside, Julia spent an hour tinkering with her bark texture until she was satisfied she could pull it off on the final cake.

She scribbled down a few ideas for creating the moss before settling on the simplest. She whisked up an egg with honey, flour, baking powder, and green food colouring before microwaving it in a mug for a minute. She shook the steaming sponge onto the counter and let it cool. With a careful hand, she ripped it up and sprinkled green specks along the base of the cake, letting it creep up the side in places. Stepping back, she smiled. Almost good enough to look for chainsaw marks.

The sound of the letterbox rattling stemmed Julia's excitement. It was half past nine in the evening, according to the oven clock. Leaving the kitchen, Julia crossed the dark café to the door, where an unmarked envelope lay on the doormat. She scooped it up and opened the door, looking toward the post office as a bundled-up figure hurried off.

"Oh no you don't." Julia put the lock on the latch and ran after them. "*Wait!*"

They spun around and pulled back their hood.

"It's all in the letter," Libbie called over her shoulder. "I didn't think you'd be there this late."

"Come to the café and talk to me. I'm getting drenched here."

Julia ran back to the café and held open the door, and after a moment's hesitation, Libbie joined her inside. Pulling down her hood, she took in the café as Julia shut the door.

"I'm not staying," she said, refusing a chair. "Like I said, it's all in the letter. What happened to your face?"

"Mask attack."

Libbie stared down at the ground as Julia ripped open the envelope. She pulled out a sheet of lined paper torn from a stationary pad.

"'Amir proposed to Flick and she turned him down. He got angry and attacked Walter with a pitchfork.'" Julia turned the letter over, but that's all she'd written. "Is Amir who you meant when you said you thought Flick would be better off with someone else?"

Libbie nodded. "They were a sweet couple. He'd come around to the house sometimes. They'd say it was just for his lessons, but they'd always have dinner and talk long into the night. He proposed to her in the summer of '89, and she turned him down. He didn't take it well."

"Why did he attack Walter with a pitchfork?"

"They got into a row at the school. Look, that's all I

know. I didn't tell you because Flick told me about the proposal in confidence. No one else knew. I promised I'd never tell anyone. He was humiliated, but after hearing about Walter, I realised I was only keeping the secret for Amir now. If he did it, I thought you'd want to know."

"From Walter to Amir," Julia said. "You said you thought Walter stole the money and framed you?"

"That's what I thought."

"If you stole the money, now would be a good time to admit it," Julia said carefully. "Molly said you were always stealing."

"What does she know?" Libbie grunted. "She came to the charity shop on Monday and she hasn't changed. Still thinks she's above it all. Said she was trying to bury the hatchet for Flick's sake. Wanted to know what I thought about the funeral, acting like butter wouldn't melt, but she wasn't an angel back then either. She was always asking Flick for money. *Always.* And she was hardly ever there. Practically lived with her dad. Look, I only came to tell you about Amir proposing, and now you know."

"Libbie, wait."

Julia reached out as Libbie pushed past her. She tried to grab her by the arm to stop her from running off, but her finger caught on something. Julia tugged her hand away, yanking off a bracelet. The string snapped, and beads bounced across the new floorboards.

"Thanks a lot," Libbie snapped. "That was my favourite."

Libbie ran off into the night. Clutching the letter and staring at the beads as they rolled into the café's corners, Julia wasn't sure what had happened, but she knew when the school reopened, she would pay a visit to Amir.

12

---

*J*ulia and Barker huddled under a golf umbrella as they walked down the lane to the school the following day. Kids in red jumpers pulled over white polo shirts ran ahead of them, tacking onto the back of the stragglers rushing to the school as the first bell of the morning rang through the halls. The gurgled electronic hum hadn't changed a note, the familiarity prickling Julia's neck hairs.

"Hurry up, Kyle," a woman called from behind them. "You can't be late again."

A small boy with white-blond hair ran around them, giving Julia a flash of déjà vu. She looked back to see a woman with an eyebrow ring scowling at Barker.

"Are you following me?" she cried as her flimsy umbrella struggled against a gust of wind. "I can't drop my grandson off at school in peace anymore?"

"Daphne," Barker remarked. "If I were following you, wouldn't I be behind you? We're here to see the groundskeeper."

"Oh, *him*."

"The man who saw you smashing Felicity's window?"

"His word against mine." Daphne clung to her umbrella's edge and tilted it into the rain. "I never did that. He needed his eyes tested."

"You confessed to my daughter."

"Did I?" She smirked. "Prove it. You can stick your investigation where the sun doesn't shine. And if I hear you've said anything to Kyle Junior, you'll regret it, Mr Brown."

"Are you threatening me?"

"Let's just say you're not the only one who can find things out."

Daphne's umbrella ripped inside out. She fought with it for a second before letting it go and setting off back down the lane. The wind ripped the brolly up above them in vicious twirls. It crashed back to earth in a mangled mess and tumbled through the rolling leaves. On the opposite side of the playground, a white gazebo shuddered amongst the trees while mud flew from the grass in a steady rhythm.

"Empty threats," Barker assured her.

"I hope so," she said, pulling open the creaking gate. "I'm not quite sure why you ruled her out. She clearly has no problem lying and backtracking. Do you think the police are the ones digging?"

"Doesn't look like them to me."

"Then it's probably Amir," Julia said. "Let's not hang around. It's freezing."

They ran past the school's front entrance, where children flowed into the assembly hall in steady lines. Under the white gazebo, Amir was knee-deep in a hole. The gazebo was doing little to protect him from the elements. He paused digging, and Julia could only imagine what they looked like from his perspective, peering down at him from underneath a giant umbrella.

"Amir Fallah?" Barker crouched down and held out his hand. Amir wiped his hand on his green overalls and gave it a single shake. "My name is Barker Brown, and this is my wife, Julia, but you've already met. You spoke with my daughter about the Felicity Campbell case. Do you have time to answer some more questions?"

Amir forced his foot down on the spade and

tossed the result over the edge. "Does it look like I have time?"

"Are you looking for the second time capsule?" Julia asked.

"As it happens, I am." Amir glanced at her, but he didn't stop digging. "I know it's around here somewhere. Since it was buried not long after Flick, I thought it might contain some evidence. Whoever put Flick in the other box must have touched this stuff to get it out."

"Not a bad idea," Barker said, handing the brolly to Julia. "Room for another?"

Julia folded Barker's trench coat over her arm while he jumped into the hole with a spade. He rolled up the sleeves of his white shirt, and after a moment's hesitation, joined Amir in digging.

"These questions?" Amir asked as they worked.

"They're about your relationship with Flick," Julia said, bending to the hole's edge. "You told Jessie that you were close friends."

"Yes, that is the truth."

"So, you *didn't* propose to her?"

"Who told you that?" Amir's foot rested on the spade. "Yes, it's true. I proposed to her."

Julia decided not to answer his question. "And she turned you down?"

"She was never going to do anything but." Amir

tossed the soil over the edge with enough force to send it past the pile. "She was the first woman who showed me kindness in this country, but I was a naïve, love-struck young man. Looking back, I know that my love was a burden on the friendship we shared, but I couldn't help but fall in love with her. I dare any person to get to know someone like Flick and not. She was a diamond, my only happiness during my early years living in this country. If I could go back, I would have kept my love to myself and let her—"

Amir's spade thudded against metal, and Barker joined him in scraping back the mud. They exposed stainless steel, the box identical to the one Julia had watched a body fall out of. She gulped as they excavated around the box, hoping someone hadn't played the same cruel trick twice. She helped Barker out of the hole and reached down with him to grab the handle. Amir's groaning suggested that the task was beyond him, but he pushed through until he was flat against the wall of the hole and the capsule was level on the grass.

Ignoring the 'To be opened in 2090' engraving, Amir bashed the spade against a rusting padlock until it gave way. He hoisted a crowbar under the rim of the lid and popped it off with a single swift kick.

No plastic sheet.

No body.

Julia let out a sigh of relief. She recognised the layout. There were seven separate boxes in a neat row, each engraved with the class from Reception to Year Six, along with the teachers' names and the names of every pupil. Julia went to find her name among the twenty or so names etched on the Year Six box, but it was the one Amir pulled out.

He dusted the mud off his hands and rummaged around in the letters and objects that hadn't seen the light of day for thirty years. He pulled out a red velvet box and fell back into the pile of soil. Tears streamed down his cheeks, tracking clean lines through the mud as he stared into the box.

"Forgive me," he said, running his filthy hands across his already dirty cheeks. "I haven't shed a tear since Flick was found. I didn't think I could. I didn't realise I was bottling them up so much, but seeing this—"

Amir's words gave way to more tears. Julia crouched next to him on the mound and wrapped an arm around his shoulders. In the velvet box, a diamond ring shone like it had been pulled from the shop display only moments ago.

"It's a beautiful ring," she said.

"Thank you. Her daughter helped me pick it out. I put it in the box on a whim. Maybe in one hundred years, when the people of the future dug it up, they'd know the story just by looking at the ring. I was so heartbroken. How could they not feel the pain trapped in this box?" He snapped the box shut and pocketed it. "How foolish we are in youth."

"It's not foolish," Julia said, "it's romantic. Did you make up with Flick after the proposal?"

"She forgave me almost immediately, though things weren't quite the same. Maybe that's why it was so easy for her to accuse me when my business loan was granted. But after I showed her my documents, we made up again. If Flick was still here today, I don't doubt we'd be best friends."

"So, you weren't humiliated?" Barker said, glancing up at the clouds as the rain finally eased. "You didn't try to attack Walter with a pitchfork?"

"My, how rumours whip around this village," Amir said, rubbing at his face with a tissue pulled from his inside pocket. "No, I didn't *attack* Walter Harkup with a pitchfork, but I know the day you're referring to. It happened before the proposal. He'd noticed how close Flick and I were growing. He warned me away from her and caused a scene in front of the parents. I was holding a rake, not a pitchfork, and I didn't attack him. He threatened to have me deported, which wasn't the first or last time someone said that to me. I gave the rake a shake. That's all. A warning to back off. He did, but then he immediately rallied everyone by saying, 'Did you see how he almost hit me?' Whose side are you going to take? He said he would press charges, but I think Flick talked him out of it."

"Only a warning swing?" Barker asked, arms folded. "Quite a stretch of the imagination to jump to rumours of a full-blown attack."

"Haven't you heard the current whispers about me on the wind?" Amir hoisted himself up with the help of a spade. "They're saying I did it, and based on what? I'm not a fool, Mr Brown. I ended up in Peridale by chance, but this community didn't welcome me with open arms when I sought asylum here. I had to prove myself, and thanks to Flick, I got to do just that. She taught me to write your language, but that was only the tip of her generosity." He stabbed the spade into the mound. A smile lifted his solemn expression. "As much as her rejection of my proposal hurt at the time, I went on to marry a woman I adored for twenty-five years. We had four sons, and I kept a good-sized roof over our heads because of my business. Despite my rough start, we had a good life. Cancer took her three years ago. Thinking about Flick's awful fate has kept me up since Bonfire Night. I'm not a violent man, Mr Brown. I fled my home country for peace. I had nothing to do with what happened to Flick."

Amir got on with his digging, turning his back to

them. Julia handed Barker his trench coat, and they set off back across the playground.

"Did you believe him?" Barker asked.

"His tears seemed real to me."

Before they could discuss it any further, a scarf waved in the air near the gate. Molly Harkup held open the gate for them, and they caught up. She clutched a takeaway cup in knit-gloved hands.

"Any updates?" Molly asked Barker eagerly before taking a sip. "I just dropped by the café to see if you were in. Delicious hot chocolate." She smiled at Julia. "Quite a nice atmosphere you've got in there. Almost didn't want to leave, but your daughter wasn't sure when you'd be back, so I'm glad I caught you."

"You weren't looking for us?" Barker asked.

"She didn't say where you'd gone, and I didn't ask." Hugging the hot chocolate, she looked wistfully at the school. "I'm afraid I've been restless at home, waiting for something to happen. They've hired a substitute to cover my classes for the next two weeks, so I'm going to put my hands to work and finish painting the sets. The children have all worked so hard rehearsing and selling tickets. It would be a shame not to let them show off." She paused as another bell rang, and Julia heard the shuffle of hundreds of tiny feet moving in the building behind them. "Perfect timing. I couldn't face the remembrance assembly. I agree it's best to face the subject head-on with the children so they can process it, but I think I'd only cause a distraction right now. Grieving is hard enough without having to answer all their big questions." She added, "Updates, Mr Brown? I saw your car outside my house last night. I was hoping you'd come with information."

"I was paying a visit to the crime scene. I did manage to talk to DI Moyes. Did she tell you about the situation with the knife?"

"Yes, quite peculiar."

"Then I don't have any concrete updates, but I have some more questions. Why didn't you mention that Amir proposed to your mother?"

"The groundskeeper?" Molly frowned. "I'm sorry, you've lost me."

"You helped him pick out the ring?"

"I did *no* such thing."

"I think he was talking about someone else," Julia whispered to Barker out of the side of her mouth. She smiled an apology to Molly, though she had questions of her own. "I spoke to Libbie last night. She said you talked to her about your mum's funeral?"

"Yes, I thought it was about time we put water under the bridge, for my mother's sake. I wanted to see if she had suggestions, but Libbie was as difficult as I remember."

"She said the same of you," Julia said without thinking. "She said you 'always' asked your mother for money and that you were hardly in the house."

"I didn't *always* ask for money," Molly said, shaking her head. "See, even now she's causing trouble. Context matters. I'd ask my mum for ten pounds here and there, twenty at the most, and only when I was short at the end of the week and needed some petrol to get around. I was a student teacher with a second job, and times were tough. She was always happy to help, and I *always* paid her back." Molly steadied herself with a breath. "And yes, I was starting to spend a lot more time at my father's house near the end, but that was *because* of Libbie. I lived through the arguments of my parents' declining marriage, only for her to show up like a tornado sent from Scotland. I was stressed enough with my studies without adding all her mischief, so yes, I avoided being around her as much as possible. But it's typical of Libbie to make out *I* was the problem. It's what Libbie has always done. She twists things to suit her."

Julia couldn't disagree. In the cold light of day – and after hearing his side of the story – Libbie's dramatic confession of Amir's proposal and pitchfork attack seemed much less significant.

Molly exhaled. "I'm sorry, it's been the week from hell, and the last thing I need is Libbie flipping my life upside down again all these years later. Do you have further questions for me?"

"Not at this time," Barker replied, stepping through the gate. "I'll be in touch as soon as I have something to tell you, but rest assured that we are coming at this from every angle."

"I appreciate it. If you can, take Saturday off." Molly reached into her bag and produced two tickets printed on thick orange cards. "I can't promise it will be the best show you've ever seen, but the kids always give it a mighty effort."

Julia accepted the tickets from the other side of the gate, and Molly set off to the school.

"Same time as Leah's wedding," Julia said, sliding them into her pocket, looking across the bonfire-scorched field to the village hall. "Maybe we can sneak out to show support. I'm sure Roxy'll want to."

"Do you really think they're going to pull off moving the wedding forward?"

"By the sounds of Johnny's text message this morning, Leah's already halfway done. She'll have planned the entire wedding before I've had the chance to finish the cake."

"The bark looks great."

"Trial run. Speaking of which, we need to get back to the café. Leah's dropping by to see how I've been getting on. I still haven't figured out edible vines. I hope the café is still quiet."

Dot's tray flew over her head, and her fresh teapot smashed against the yellow paint as she tumbled backwards. Jessie hurried over, but Evelyn dove in and caught Dot before she hit the table behind her. The tray fell from her hands and clattered to a stop on the table. In the silence, nobody moved or said a word.

"I saw that coming," Evelyn said, breaking the silence. "Here, Dorothy, you need them more than me right now."

"Forget mysticism!" Dot cried, batting away Evelyn's hands as she tried to wrap crystal necklaces around her. "In the here and now, I could have broken my neck. I could have died. I could *sue!*"

"Surely you wouldn't sue Julia, Dot?" Jessie said.

"Shock can make us say things we don't mean." Evelyn tried to force Dot into a chair, but she didn't bend. "You should sit down. You nearly had a terrible fall."

"I said I *could* sue, so it's a good thing that I'm family. Julia might not have been so lucky if this café had belonged to someone else." Dot tugged free of

Evelyn. "And thank you for saving me, Evelyn, but I didn't fall. I *slipped*." She snapped to the ground and straightened back up with something pinched between her fingers. "Why are there *balls* on the floor?"

"Oh my," Evelyn muttered.

"Tiny wooden balls." Dot pointed across the café. "There's another one there. And there."

Jessie crouched to look at the wooden balls, phone in hand. She pulled up the picture she'd taken at Walter Harkup's crime scene. They weren't identical, but it was strange to find similar ones in the café.

"Ah, Julia!" Dot exclaimed as the bell rang. "I almost slipped to my death. Suppose it hadn't been for Evelyn's *third* eye, you'd currently be looking at your grandmother spread across this table with a broken spine and a glassy look in her eyes, wondering why you'd turned your café into a death trap."

"Wooden balls," Jessie said, tossing one to Julia.

"Ah. I thought I'd swept them all up."

"Where did they come from?" Jessie asked, handing Julia the brush. "They look like the ones I saw at the crime scene."

"I caught Libbie's bracelet when she was here yesterday. Beads burst everywhere. They blend in with the floorboards. I'm sorry, Gran."

"Yes, well, no harm done," Dot said, adjusting her brooch. "And I'm sorry about the teapot. I hope you still have some paint left." Dot blinked at her. "What happened to your face, Julia? You're as red as a beetroot."

Once all the beads and broken porcelain were swept up, Jessie took a break, leaving Julia to fact-check Dot's account of her near-death experience to the newcomers. Given her exhilaration as Jessie left, anyone would think her slip had taken place on a cliff's edge. Not wanting to waste a second, Jessie set off to Mulberry Lane.

A police car was parked outside the charity shop. Jessie set off at a jog. The door opened while Jessie was still two shops away, and a pair of officers dragged Libbie out. The rattling beaded necklaces and bracelets gave her away.

"It was you," Jessie said. "You killed them."

"Please don't talk to her," DI Moyes ordered as she left the charity shop. "Get her in the car."

Libbie thrashed against their hold, but they managed to force her into the back of the car. Her hair over her face, she screamed and kicked the back of the front seats. Mulberry Lane had come to a standstill as shoppers stopped to watch the street theatre.

"The beads?" Jessie asked.

"Yes, the beads." DI Moyes unlocked her car further up the street. "They were covered in her DNA, and we pulled perfect prints from the knife. Still had them on file from her last arrest. Tell your dad there are no hard feelings. There are some cases only good old-fashioned police work can solve."

"Tell him yourself."

DI Moyes followed the police car away from Mulberry Lane, with Libbie thrashing and screaming the whole way. While the street erupted into gossipy whispers as the cars turned out of view, Jessie stared through the charity shop window. More beaded jewellery hung on racks on the counter. Had it really all come down to a bracelet and a fingerprint?

After all her digging, Jessie had expected a more exciting conclusion to the murders of Felicity Campbell and Walter Harkup.

13

A nearby death was always sure to fill the café, but so was an arrest.

After Jessie's frenzied return with news of Libbie's capture, villagers filed through the door until there was no room to stand, let alone sit. For once, Julia wished she was sitting in a café instead of running one because it would have given her time to absorb what was happening. With the gossip all grossly speculative, there wasn't much news to glean from the conversation. When it came time to close, Julia was happy to wave her gran through the door and flip the sign behind her. Before she could lock up, DI Moyes' car stopped next to the green.

"Not too late for another hot chocolate, am I?"

"Yes," Dot answered on her way home. "Good job on catching her. Took you long enough."

Julia stepped aside to let the DI in. She locked the door behind her and pulled down the blind before whipping up one of Jessie's hot chocolates. She opted for a mug instead of a takeaway cup, and topped it with a generous swirl of cream and marshmallows, hoping to entice the DI to stay for a conversation. Barker had said something about her preferring cream over fruit cake.

"Congratulations," Julia said. "Jessie said it was the DNA."

"Never fails." Moyes accepted Julia's offer of the chair at the table nearest the counter. "Well, mostly never fails. Libbie insists that she's been framed, but we're not falling for that a second time."

Julia wished she had made herself a drink to sip, to hide her puckering lips. DI Moyes grinned and scooped up some of the cream with her finger.

"What's the bee in your bonnet buzzing about, Julia? This is a closed case. Two crimes, thirty years apart, one print-covered knife."

"Well, if Libbie was framed the first time, what's to say it's not happening again?" The thought had been bugging Julia in the back of her mind since the arrest. "After all the first framing was done well enough to result in a charge."

"Which the forged letters cleared her of." Moyes plucked off a marshmallow. "Didn't you think it was curious that the letters were responsible for that? If any of the others had done it, why would they have bothered to absolve Liberty in the process? If the aim was to keep their charity money secret, they could have let the truth die with Felicity and let Liberty rot. She's the only one invested in her innocence."

"Okay," Julia said, nodding, "What do you think happened? Libbie claimed she last saw Felicity the night before she died. I don't know how methanol poisoning works exactly, but she was alive and well the following morning and into the afternoon."

"Libbie obviously met up with Felicity on the day to administer the poison," Moyes said. "I believe Felicity found some concrete proof against Libbie that would secure her conviction in 1989. Perhaps Felicity did try to extract a confession from Libbie the night before. One last stab at getting the truth. When that didn't work, Libbie realised her days were numbered. She poisoned Felicity, found her at the school, improvised, and you were there to see the result thirty years later."

"The letters?"

"She would have had easy access to samples and months to practice. Going to Scotland would have broken her bail conditions, but she still had connections. Parents. Siblings. What's to say she didn't post the letters up there for them to send back?"

"Interesting theory," Julia agreed with a nod. "Libbie did mention that she wasn't close to any of them. She resents her parents for abandoning her, and apparently, her siblings weren't on her side in the fallout."

"Then she broke her bail and caught the train up there," Moyes said with a dry laugh. "There's no way to know unless she tells us, but she's fallen back on 'no comment.' You know she said that all through her first interviews back in '89 too?" Leaning back in her chair, she smiled. "You know, they were wrong about you at the station."

"Do I want to know?"

"They have this impression that you enjoy sticking your nose in," Moyes continued. "Maybe they're right, but I can see you care about justice. And you said I was tenacious. It's admirable. It's why I got into policing in the first place. Can I have this in a takeaway cup? I did only come for the hot chocolate."

Julia drowned the cream and marshmallows as she transferred the drink to a paper cup. She slid it across the counter, and Moyes pulled out her card to pay.

"On the house," Julia said. "I hope you're right about this. I have a wedding cake and a dessert buffet to pull together, and it would be nice to give it my full attention."

"Then you do that." Moyes set off to the door. She paused and asked, "This wedding? Is it that teacher friend of yours with the red hair?"

"No. Why?"

"No reason." Moyes lifted the cup above her head. "Thanks for the drink. Rest easy, Julia. The case is over."

"Think about it," Jessie said as she paced in front of the investigation board in the office downstairs. "It all makes sense. Libbie tried to blame Walter, and the second she stabbed him, she made Amir her target. She killed Felicity because Felicity figured out the truth about the money, and then she killed Walter to keep the secret."

Jessie could tell Barker wasn't convinced. He'd been watching the record spin around with little to say.

"What did Walter find out?" Barker posed. "How did he know it was Libbie?"

"Whatever secret Felicity found out. Some piece of evidence. I don't know. What else could have happened?"

The door at the top of the stairs opened, and Julia joined them, hopefully, to bring some sense to the room – especially once she revealed she'd just had a conversation with DI Moyes.

"Libbie thinks she was framed?" Barker said, leaning back in his creaky chair. "That's where my mind has gone too. The knife. Why was the knife different?"

"Maybe she stabbed him with one and then gave it another go with another?" Jessie shrugged. "Why would her DNA be at the crime scene if she wasn't been there?"

"There are many ways," Barker said knowingly. "She worked in a shop. She's always touching things. DNA transference is happening all around you."

"Do they sell knives in charity shops?" Jessie asked. "Mum, you went."

"I didn't notice any, but I also wasn't looking."

"They do sell beads," Jessie admitted. "On racks on the counter. Libbie clearly likes them. She could have tried them on and put them back, and she probably stocked them. Would that be enough to put her DNA on them?"

"Now you're getting it," Barker said with a nod. "And why would Libbie go to all the trouble of killing Felicity with methanol when she could have just stabbed her like Walter? Poisoning Felicity makes no sense unless she just happened to have methanol on her. Now, I've been researching methanol, and it has so many uses it's difficult to pin it down to a particular place, but some things cropped up. You can spray methanol on plants to help them grow, so Amir could get his hands on it easily. It's also used in car paint. Molly and Daphne worked in a car factory. Libbie was fifteen. Did she really go to all that trouble pulling off getting away with murder for all these years?"

"Mum?" Jessie prompted, pulling Julia from her silent trance at the board. "What are you thinking?"

"Libbie and Felicity were close," she said. "Close enough that Amir trusted Libbie to help pick out a ring. He referred to Libbie as Felicity's daughter. Libbie had one family turn their backs on her. It doesn't make sense that she'd go this far to betray someone she looked to as a mother."

"People can be self-destructive creatures," Jessie said.

"But poisoning?" Julia walked to the desk and picked up Barker's methanol research. "Decreased level of consciousness, poor coordination, irritation of the eyes, vomiting, abdominal pain, hypothermia, blindness." Julia paused and blinked tears down her cheeks. She quickly whipped them away. "It's a horrible way to die. Could Libbie have put Felicity through that? A knife between the shoulder blades would have been easier."

"Someone did," Jessie said. "If not Libbie, who?"

"Like I said, Daphne, Molly, and Amir all had access to the poison." Barker joined Jessie at the board. "And we can't trust anything Daphne has said. Even if her alibi is true, karaoke started at eight, so there's still an hour unaccounted for. Not to mention that she's completely backpedalled on her confession and is back to saying Amir needs an eye test."

"Great," Jessie said with a huff. "So, just to recap, if it wasn't Libbie, it could have been any of them? Mum? Who's your money on?"

Julia stared at the board without giving an answer. She stepped forward and pulled down one of the notes – Amir's witness statement saying he'd waved to Felicity as she ran across the playground.

"Mum?"

"Eye irritation and blindness," Julia said, tapping the card up and down against her palm. "Could that have been what Amir saw? He said her eyes were streaming, and she didn't see him."

"Well, if it wasn't Libbie," Jessie said, tossing her arms out, "what aren't *we* seeing?"

14

-----

*P*reparations for the wedding kept Julia so busy over the next few days that she had no choice but to trust the police had arrested the right suspect. Just like the wedding cake, the dessert buffet was a more significant undertaking than Julia had anticipated.

With the arrest keeping the café busy as the week peaked, Julia spent every free moment between customers planning what she wanted to make for the evening's dessert buffet. Running around with her own mountain of tasks, Leah approved everything after the first plan was emailed. She also included a post-script asking if Julia could make twenty-five desserts for the final course of the wedding breakfast. Against her better judgement, Julia replied with an assurance that she could. After spending ten minutes on the kitchen's back doorstep, staring out at the field behind the café, she wondered how she could fit another task into the wedding day schedule. In the end, she decided that she wouldn't, and in need of something she could pre-make and that someone else could efficiently serve, she was glad Leah approved of crème brûlée.

On Friday, Jessie manned the café on her own, leaving Julia to bury herself in the kitchen. The morning and much of the afternoon were spent pulling together all her tests to create the final wedding cake. Then she baked all the cakes for the buffet. The mountain of washing up never shrank despite how often they attacked it with sinks of soapy water. It was the kind of day that begged Julia to spend the rest of her evening with her feet in front of the fire, a hot water bottle crammed behind her back.

Once they were closed, Julia tossed back an espresso shot and promised Jessie they'd clean the café on Sunday. Not every day was the day before the wedding of two of her closest friends. So special, she put a quickly scribbled 'CLOSED FOR WEDDING' sign in the door on her way out. There wasn't much she'd close her café on a Saturday for.

"Oh, Julia, thank goodness you're here." Leah

hugged her tightly as she walked into the village hall. "There's still so much to do."

The village hall mess made Julia forget about the day she'd had in the café. She'd be there all night. Plastic carrier bags bursting with decorations sat on half a dozen round tables. A team of four was in the process of putting in a dancefloor, and two more were constructing a lighting rig around the room, trailing wires everywhere.

Rolling up her sleeves, Julia asked Leah where she wanted her. After being handed an instruction booklet, Julia spent the next hour assembling artificial white birch trees. The first was fiddly, the second less so, and she didn't need the instructions by the third. They fit together like something between a hatstand and a naked Christmas tree. By the time she'd finished assembling a dozen trees, the exposed cement brick walls of the village hall had been covered in backlit pleated white fabric. As Leah used the remote to tinker with the lighting behind them, flicking between gold and red, Julia could see the vision coming together. Roxy joined them after the bar and DJ booth had been installed.

"Major cognitive dissonance," Roxy said, lingering at the door. "I *know* I just walked into the village hall, but where on earth am I?" She popped her head back out and checked the outside. "Brilliant. No wonder this is your job, Leah."

"It's coming together."

"Coming together? You've built a room in a room." Roxy shrugged off her coat and joined them at the table where they were inserting AAA batteries into LED candles. "Sorry I'm so late. Molly needed every pair of hands to help finish painting the sets. We lost too many days."

"How's she doing?" Julia asked.

"Better since the arrest. The whole school seems more peaceful. I know it's down to the hot case being extinguished, but a part of me can't help but wonder if it's because Harkup isn't stalking the halls anymore. Where do you want me, Leah?"

With only string lights to wrap around wreaths, they finished within half an hour of Roxy's arrival. They stuffed the rubbish from their package-ripping into black bags, tossed them in the bins outside, and shut off the lights.

"I'm getting married tomorrow," Leah said quietly as the three looked around the darkened autumn wonderland. "This wasn't my first time transforming a village hall, but never in four days. I can't believe we pulled it off."

"How about another spa night at Julia's, so we're all looking our best?" Roxy asked as Leah closed the doors, locking them up. "Julia's redness has finally gone down."

"Only took a few days."

"I'll join you later," Leah said, waving as she jogged to her car. "Katie's squeezed me in for nails, and I'm getting my roots touched up at the same time by my hairdresser."

"At nine o'clock at night?" Roxy said.

"I'm a big tipper," she said, half in her car. "I've been meaning to ask, Rox. I wasn't sure whether to set a place for Violet. Did she get back to you?"

"Oh." Roxy's cheeks prickled as red as her hair. "She can't make it. Family stuff still. She sends her apologies."

Roxy's response was enough to get Leah into her car and off for her last-minute touch-ups, but Julia was far from satisfied. She'd seen her best friend dodging the question enough times now to feel confident that something had happened between the couple. Once they were in the car and driving up the quiet lane to Julia's cottage, she knew she couldn't sit on it any longer.

"It's not 'family stuff', is it?"

Julia glanced at Roxy, but her friend turned to the window as they passed the construction sight of James Jacobson's slowly advancing house.

"Technically, it is," Roxy said, still looking away.

"As in, she's gone back to her family in Russia. We broke up at the beginning of the summer."

"Beginning of *summer*?" Julia ground the car to a halt halfway to her cottage. She locked the handbrake and turned to Roxy. "You broke up with Violet that long ago and haven't said anything?"

"Technically, she broke up with me."

"Oh, Roxy."

"I didn't want to put a downer on things." Blinking up at the car's metal ceiling, she exhaled. "You had your baby, and Johnny and Leah had just got engaged. Her work visa came up for renewal, and the next thing I knew, we were having 'the talk'. Not on the same page, grown apart, want different things, and the rest. It blindsided me. Thankfully, I had the summer holidays to straighten myself out. If I'd had to go through that at school, I might have gone on a Miss Campbell spiral, shaved my head, and started arguing with everyone I knew. I hid away in my flat and got through it, and the more time I spent alone there, the more I realised that nobody had noticed what I was going through. My sister's in prison, Mum's losing more of her mind every year, and my friends had all moved on."

The words stung.

"I never moved on from you, Roxy."

"I know that now, but have you never been in that

place, Julia? Stuck on the sofa thinking nothing matters and your life is over? I spent my summer like a Victorian widow waiting for her husband to return from the war." Roxy rested her hand atop Julia's on the steering wheel. Julia remembered those days all too well. She'd been divorced. "I'm not blaming you. Or Johnny, or Leah, or anyone. Truth be told, I don't think I knew how to be friends with someone with a baby. I know how silly that sounds, given my job, but they're kids. They're different. When have I ever been around babies?"

"It's still me, Rox."

"And now I've had the chance to see that, which is why I feel like a wally." Roxy squeezed Julia's hand, and they shared a smile. "If it means anything, I was going to tell you all after the wedding. But my love life was the last thing Leah needed to be thinking about, especially with how things have gone."

"But you could have told me."

"I should have. You'd have helped drag me out of the slump way quicker. You're like a human bath bomb. You made me feel relaxed. Good news is, you're getting me six months post-break-up, so I'm showered and speaking in coherent sentences again ... most of the time. Like the wedding, it all turned out for the best in the end, which won't happen to us if you don't get a move on. That bus is about to hit us head-on, and I think the death of her two bridesmaids might just be the thing to send Leah over the edge."

At Dot and Percy's cottage, Jessie won another round of poker, claiming the pile of chocolate buttons. Percy had already folded and was in the armchair reading the paper in the lamp's glow.

"When did you get so good?" Dot pouted, shuffling the cards for their next game.

"What do you think me and Alfie did in all those airports?"

"It's nice to finally have a worthy opponent. No offence, dear."

"None was taken, my love." Percy chuckled, turning the page. "I say, this Liberty Turner sounds like a handful. Makes you wonder how these people put so little value on life that they're willing to murder two people for a few thousand pounds. You'd think they'd have given up the ghost by now."

"Yes, well, the ghosts have been set free now that the truth is out, or so Evelyn says." Dot stopped her shuffling and moved on to dealing the cards. "We can all sleep easy again knowing they have the culprit behind bars. I often go to that charity shop on Mulberry Lane. Libbie's always given me a funny feeling. Shifty eyes. You can tell these sorts of things. I knew it was her from the start."

"You thought it was Amir."

"He was *one* of my suspects."

Jessie decided against bringing up Dot's hour-long performance at the café.

"Do you really think it's all over?"

"Why wouldn't it be?" Dot jabbed a finger at the paper as Percy turned the pages. Her gaze lingered on the clunky radio box covered in dials and flashing lights in the corner, and not for the first time that night. "The headline says it all. 'THEY HAD HER THIRTY YEARS AGO!' Walter might not have been the nicest of men, but he'd still be here if they'd done their jobs properly. It's absurd that they shut down the search for Felicity based on a sleepy old man's analysis." Dot's chin vanished into her neck as she checked her cards close to the table. "Your father has wrapped up his investigation, I presume?"

"Putting together a final report for Molly, but he's not convinced Libbie did it. He said he'd have expected her to crack and confess by now, but she's still claiming she's innocent."

"And they'd be fools to believe her. Shifty eyes, remember."

Jessie decided not to push the case anymore. After tying the beads to Libbie, she'd been sure they'd found their murderer, but Barker's doubts had poisoned the waters. She'd hoped Dot and Percy would offer a different perspective outside the same story she'd heard in the café on a circle for two days, but their comments were the generic stock parroted from the paper.

"Speaking of shifty eyes, you keep looking at that giant old-school radio," Jessie pointed out. "It's taking up half the room. Where'd you get it?"

"Do I?" Dot said airily with a waft of her hand. "It's vintage. Picks up ... special channels."

"Like other countries?"

"Like other countries." Dot glanced at Percy as he hid behind his paper. Snatching up her cards, Dot pushed forward a sickly sweet smile that didn't quite suit her. "Now, time for me to win back my chocolate buttons before the night disappears."

"Johnny, we shouldn't be seeing each other the night before the wedding," Leah said in the hallway. "It's bad luck."

"We've had our bad luck. Who am I supposed to spend the night before my wedding with, if not my three best friends?"

"Julia, shimmy over," Roxy instructed in the sitting

room, and Julia shuffled further into the corner of the sofa. "Leah, let the man in from the rain. There's room for one more."

Johnny and Leah joined them under the duvet, and Julia tossed Johnny a pair of bed socks, of which she had a drawer full. He settled, adding his pink and white socks to the row of four already on the coffee table, toasting in front of the fire. Roxy unpaused *Bridesmaids* and Kristen Wiig continued sashaying down the aeroplane aisle in black sunglasses on the screen.

"Doesn't this feel like one of our teenage sleepovers?" Leah said.

"Except Roxy hasn't pulled out a bottle of cider," Johnny corrected, "and you haven't tried to read us our horoscopes."

"I was going through a phase."

"Remember your horse phase?" Roxy said. "And your too-short-fringe phase?"

"We all had that phase." Julia could practically feel the cold metal of her gran's kitchen scissors above her brows. "But you're right. It does feel like one of our sleepovers."

"Except we're all in our forties and should probably have pillows behind our backs. We can't afford the slouching." Roxy patted Julia on the arm and pointed over the sofa arm. "Grab that plastic bag.

I was going to leave this until tomorrow. But, since we're all here talking about old times, the groundskeeper dug up the 'official' time capsule, and I had a little dig through and found what we put in."

Roxy emptied out the bag on the duvet and passed out their things. Julia hadn't been able to visualise what her handwritten recipe book had looked like. Still, now that the stapled pages were in her hands, she couldn't believe she'd forgotten. Her mum had drawn a chocolate cake, but she'd coloured it in with felt tips so dark, the cake resembled a brick. After a blank page to account for the felt tip bleeding, there was a short passage explaining that Julia was an eleven-year-old girl who lived in Peridale, and her 'favourite thing in the whole world was baking'.

Some things never changed.

The recipes were all simple, but a couple were on the café's menu, unchanged. The recipes were based wholly on her mother's, so the Victoria sponge and chocolate cake were written exactly as Julia still made them today. Her mother had written the titles for each item at the top of every page, and Julia had penned the ingredients and steps in a squiggly parody of her mother's perfect scrawl. Julia's handwriting hadn't evolved into anything as graceful as her mother's but she was surprised by how much their writing had in common.

"I put in this framed dried rose," Leah said, holding it up to show them. "I didn't know what to put in, so my mum gave me this. She went through her own phase, pressing roses and giving them out as gifts. I'll miss her tomorrow."

Julia smiled at the memory of Emily Burns, her first neighbour across the lane when she'd moved into her cottage. As much as Leah tried, the rose bushes had never been as immaculate as when her late mother tended to them.

"I put in some pictures I took around Peridale," Johnny said, flicking through a stack of glossy six-by-fours. "I thought I was being artsy, but they're all badly composed shots of lifeless countryside in November with no subject. Julia?"

"Handwritten recipe book. Wrote it with my mum. Rox?"

"I wrote *myself* a letter," Roxy said, her lips raising a smile as she cleared her throat. "'Hello, future Roxy in 2090. Miss Campbell said we'll all be dead by then, but I don't believe her. They're going to figure out a way that we can all live forever, so I just wanted to say hi. I hope you're living in a massive house with lots of money and every VHS and cassette tape you want. Say hi to Julia for me. And Johnny and Leah. Are you all floating heads in jars in the future? That would be cool. I'm running out of space now. I hope you're happy. Love from, Past Roxy, aged eleven.'" Roxy folded the letter, and Julia was touched by her friend's past words. "My eleven-year-old self says hi."

"Hi," they replied in unison.

Their laughter died down, and when the reminiscing faded, they were left with the comfortable silence that only old friends could enjoy together. With the credits of *Bridesmaids* rolling, Julia didn't want the moment to end. She was all too aware that this could be one of the last nights they were all together in Peridale.

Like all good things, the silence couldn't last. Johnny's phone pinged in his pocket. He threw back the duvet, letting out the warmth, and wriggled it out. He scanned a short message before jumping off the sofa.

"Libbie's being released without charge. I need to go."

Julia's heart skipped a beat.

"Released?" Julia sat upright. "When?"

"It's happening right now." Johnny hobbled into a shoe, knocking into the lamp. Leah steadied it. "Iron-clad alibi, according to my source."

"Why now?" Leah groaned. "I thought we were over this."

"Libbie must be innocent." Johnny's messenger bag went over his head as he hopped, putting on the other shoe. "I won't be able to cover it tomorrow. I need to get something done tonight. Leah, I love you, and I can't wait for you to become Mrs Watson."

"Don't work too late," she called after him. With just the three of them, they all nudged in closer to the middle, now three pairs of bed socks in a row. "There's still a killer out there. Who could it be?"

"I don't know," Julia admitted. "What do we do?"

"We make a tough decision," Leah said, plucking the remote from Roxy's lap. "*Bad Moms* or *A Bad Moms Christmas*?"

Julia tried to focus as Leah flicked between the two near-identical films on the screen, but her mind was already flipping through the notepad she'd left on the kitchen counter.

Rest easy, DI Moyes had said.

Julia couldn't believe she'd listened.

15

*J*ulia could feel the elephant in the room as she stirred the following morning. Leah's chirpy voice floated from the kitchen, as did the scent of something sweet and buttery that instantly made her hungry. Julia rolled over to Barker's side of the bed. He was already up, and Mowgli was spread out on his back in the dent in the mattress.

"Mustn't mention the case," she whispered to Mowgli, tickling his belly. "Mustn't let the fact there's a murderer on the loose get in the way of Leah and Johnny's big day."

Leah being Leah, she'd planned everything down to the last detail, so naturally, freshly made Belgian waffles greeted Julia when she sat next to Roxy on the breakfast bar. Barker was by the oven, and Leah was helping Olivia rip up her toast.

"Morning," Barker said, kissing her from behind, toothpaste fresh on his breath. "Sleep well?"

Julia looked at the man by the oven, whose only resemblance to Barker was his dark hair. How late had they stayed up talking last night that she'd mistaken the stranger for Barker? He served Roxy a plate of fresh pancakes topped with cream and strawberries and produced a glass of champagne for Julia.

"I could get used to this," Roxy mumbled through a mouthful of pancakes as she stabbed at the strawberries one after the other. "Champagne with breakfast? What's not to love?"

"Go easy on the fizz, Rox. You have a speech to give." Leah pulled out her binder and cracked it open. "If you need help with your speech, I made a light framework you can plug things into."

"What do you think I do all day? Teaching is long-form improv to a room full of kids with goldfish attention spans. I have to do backflips to get them to focus on simple multiplication and division these days. A wedding speech will be a piece of cake."

"Just be honest," Leah said, closing her binder. "But maybe not too honest."

"I'll speak from the heart. Relax, Leah. You've earned it."

The mystery chef who'd taken over Julia's kitchen was only the first of a revolving crew of professionals. The hair and make-up team came in as the chef left, followed by the dressmakers with the finished pieces after last-minute alterations. Their introductions were polite head nods, each getting straight to work like they could hear the clock ticking a little louder than everyone else.

When Julia had on a base of foundation and her naturally curly hair was blow-dried smooth and stacked into gigantic Velcro rollers, Leah informed her it was the perfect time for her to move the wedding cake from the café to the village hall.

"I'm the only one not double dipping in this wedding," Roxy said, spread out in the armchair in the corner of Julia's bedroom, helping herself to a dish of strawberries. She plucked a scarf off the back of the chair and tossed it to Julia. "It's windy out there."

Julia's old car wobbled against the gale as she drove down the lane to the village. She parked in her usual spot, and with the scarf knotted at her chin, she ran around to the back of the cafe and into the kitchen. The wedding cake greeted her on the island, four tiers of autumnal perfection, if she said so herself. The bottom two layers were the pumpkin spice fruit cake. The top two were a lighter cinnamon sponge, with vanilla buttercream and winter berry jam sandwiched between the layers. Multi-tonal leaves spiralled around the cake like the wind had whipped up them up, but they might tumble back to the ground at any moment. It had taken an hour of adding and removing the delicate fondant leaves to create such ordered chaos, and the same went for the placement of the moss and vines. Julia was glad she'd taken every second. She pulled out her notepad and flicked back to the wedding cake checklist. At the bottom, under 'Assemble and decorate', she added 'Be proud and marvel at work' and added a big tick next to it.

Holding the pad, Julia was drawn to her most recent notes, hastily made in bed the night before. Too tired to dive into the details, her scribbles amounted to wanting to talk to Libbie and DI Moyes as soon as possible. She needed to know what had led to her release. She'd been itching to ask Johnny what he'd found out after running off the night before, but for the same reason she hadn't brought it up with Leah, she couldn't bring herself to call.

After checking on the fridge overflowing with buffet items and the shelves of crème brûlée, Julia packed the cake in a box. Clinging to the box like her life depended on it, she walked backwards down the alley, into the wind. Julia didn't take a breath until the cake was in the front seat with the seatbelt across it.

She drove around the green as slowly as possible and crawled to a halt outside the church. Thankfully, the DJ was at the village hall to hold open the doors and offer her help carrying the cake to the buffet table.

"That's sick," the DJ said when Julia tugged away the box. She pulled out her phone and took a picture, the highest praise. "Props to whoever made it."

With a promise that Julia would pass her 'props' on, she left the village hall. Jessie, Barker, Dot, and Roxy had all seen the cake and assured her it was perfect, but there was nothing like an unprompted compliment from a stranger. Julia's warm fuzzy glow lasted as long as it took her to walk to the church gates. DI Moyes' car was parked at the top of the school lane.

"Detective," she called, waving as Moyes climbed out of her car. "Have you got a moment to talk about the case?"

"Whoever you are, whatever it is, it'll need to wait," she called back, holding up a hand as she set off with vast strides.

"It's Julia."

"Julia?" Moyes stopped and squinted, backtracking a couple of steps. "With pale face and rollers under a scarf, I thought you were another of the local old lady mafia hounding me for answers."

"I'm halfway cooked," she said. "Wedding."

"And yet you've still found time to hunt me down." The detective looked down the lane to the school, but she took a step closer to Julia. "What is it? I'm a little busy."

"Libbie was released with all charges dropped?"

"It would seem she was telling the truth about being framed," Moyes admitted with a tight smile. "Regretfully, I believed the evidence put before me, but it was staged rather well."

"The knife and the beads?"

Moyes nodded. "After further investigation, we've confirmed the knife came from a set on the charity shop's shelf."

"And it's easy enough to slip beads into a pocket," Julia thought aloud. "Why did it take so long to confirm her alibi?"

"Libbie claimed she was babysitting her next-door neighbour's kid. She said it was the first time, and we couldn't track down her neighbour. She's a single mum with two jobs and was wary of answering the door to the police. Thought we were there because she's been stealing Libbie's Wi-Fi for years. She got in touch when she saw the article in the paper. The regular childminder cancelled at the last minute, and Libbie stepped in and offered. Said Libbie had given her a teddy for the child a few days before. Good thing for Libbie that she didn't trust her because it meant she turned on her nanny camera. Libbie played imaginary tea parties with the kid, read her to sleep, and then spent the rest of the night cleaning the flat. Wouldn't let her neighbour pay her and offered to do it any time. Turns out she's quite charitable."

Just like Flick.

"I was at the charity shop when she was picking out the teddy. She said she could hear the little girl crying and wanted to help."

"Look, I already feel bad enough." Moyes exhaled. "When someone has a record, it's easier to believe when the dots of a new crime scene seem to connect."

"But are you closer to proving who's been leaving these dots?"

"We're following some—"

"Interesting lines of inquiry?" Julia jumped in, arching a brow. "You must have something solid?"

"This can't get out," Moyes said, glancing around the village. Dot and Percy were walking their dogs on the green, and all four sets of eyes were staring at them. "We found some rogue fibres in the capsule Felicity was buried in. They weren't part of her clothes, but there were fibres of everything floating around all the time, so they were excluded as an anomaly. When the groundskeeper dug up the second capsule, we found those same fibres among some of the capsule boxes."

"What kind of fibres?"

"Fabric," Moyes said, backing away from Julia and glancing at the green. "If this is what I think it is, the case will be over before the end of the day. Focus on the wedding, Julia. Your hands are clearly as full as your hair."

DI Moyes set off down the lane as Dot and Percy hurried in, fur coats keeping them half a metre apart.

"Crikey, Julia! You look like someone's granny!"

"DI Moyes already beat you to it."

Dot pursed her lips toward the lane, craning her neck to watch the DI's journey. "And what did she have to say for herself now that the case is circling the drain?"

"She seems to think it could be over today."

"That'll be the handwriting analysis," Percy said confidently. "The latest development eliminates the groundskeeper."

"Latest development?"

"The letters were forged by a *woman*," Dot whispered. "There's at least a seventy percent chance of it. They can figure out all sorts of things these days."

"Where did you hear that?"

"Oh, just in the air," Dot said, pushing up her

curls. "But from where I'm standing, that only leaves two people. The daughter and the angry mother."

Molly and Daphne.

The two names circled around Julia's mind the whole drive back to her cottage. As much as she wanted to sit in her car thinking about the case, she'd already exceeded the time Leah had allotted for cake transportation.

Taking a deep breath at the front door, Julia entered with a smile as a photographer's flash blinded her. She hoped Leah couldn't hear the ticking of the grenade from which DI Moyes had pulled the pin.

The wedding ceremony went the same as every wedding Jessie had ever been to. The priest talked for too long while people stared gooey-eyed at the bride and groom, snivelling into their tissues – though that could have been from how cold the church was. Even though she'd known her wedding would be in November, Leah had gone backless with her dress, not that you could tell she was cold. She grinned from ear to ear through the entire thing, and when Father David pronounced them man and wife and it came time for their first kiss, Jessie was sure she saw a breath of relief leave both newlyweds.

Given how their luck had gone so far, Jessie had expected an escaped lion from the zoo to rampage through the church while the village flooded. Luckily for Leah and Johnny, the wedding ended the same way every wedding did, with kisses and congratulations, all wrapped up in confetti and followed by overly posed pictures.

Jessie posed for the first round of pictures, but she snuck out through the church gates when the photographer started using the phrase 'and now let's take a silly one' every other picture.

Jessie returned to Barker's office, where she'd spent her morning. From the sounds of it, she'd been the only one to get an early night, and she'd only read about Libbie's release on the *Peridale Chat* group that morning.

Settling into the well-worn chair behind the desk, Jessie picked up the defunct report her dad had written to detail Libbie's guilt. She flicked through the pages, but her eyes were on their notes. No one had added to them since the night of Libbie's arrest, yet she'd found Barker staring at them on each visit. Flicking on the vinyl player as she crossed the room, Jessie did the same. Her eyes locked on the same note she'd been focusing on all morning.

The hour following lunch at the pub.

According to Barker's research, methanol

poisoning, while lethal, didn't display its effects immediately. It could take a few hours at least, a whole day at most. In the report, he'd suggested Libbie could have administered the poison during the meeting the day before Felicity was murdered.

But with Libbie out of the picture, the hour before she was seen crying had to be too late for the poisoning to have taken place when she'd been in such 'high spirits' at four. She must have been displaying some symptoms over lunch, yet Molly had said she'd gone over the lunch several times to look for signs. Jessie set off from her dad's office and down the path leading to the school.

"Miss Harkup?" the receptionist said, checking the guestbook on the table – nothing more than an open book with a pen. "She's not signed in today, and I haven't seen her. The play isn't due to start until six, and the children aren't getting here to start rehearsing until half past four. She's sure to be here by then. Can I take a name?"

Jessie gave her name, and she flicked back through the pages of the guestbook to the Sunday night of Walter's murder. Molly's two entries were the only logs for the day. She arrived at 5:00 pm and left at 11:30 pm.

"Does anyone ever check this?" Jessie asked before she left. "To make sure it's true?"

"I'm not sure I'm following you, dear."

"Well, anyone could write anything in here," she said, picking up the pen and scribbling in the book. "According to this, I came here on Sunday at one in the afternoon and never left."

"But I *saw* you write that," the lady said with an unsure laugh. "I think I get what you're asking. No, it's not verified. I tell everyone to sign it on their way in and out, but do you think they listen? And besides, as far as I know, nobody was here on Sunday."

"How would you know?"

"Because the school was still being picked apart by the forensic team until Monday afternoon, and nobody could get in. Unless they were helping with the investigation, nobody was here. People are always writing down the wrong dates. Easily done."

"But it's her alibi."

"Whose alibi for what, dear?" She peered over the glasses perched on the end of her nose. "Why did you say you wanted to speak with Miss Harkup? You look a little young to have a student in her class."

"I didn't say." Jessie stared through the blinds at the tree fighting against the wind, drumming her fingers on the book. "Don't suppose you know which bus goes to Riverswick?"

Jessie left the school and hurried past the church to the bus stop outside the post office. The photographer was still dragging the group around the church's grounds, swapping out people for different configurations. However, from the thinning numbers, she wasn't the only one who'd snuck away.

She checked her watch as the bus pulled up.

She'd miss the wedding breakfast, but she'd make it back for the reception. Enough time to get to Riverswick, talk to Molly about the exact details of her alibi, and back again in time for cake-cutting and dancing couples. She'd never been the biggest fan of speeches and crème brûlée anyway.

Unlike the direct bus to Fern Moore, the 545 to Riverswick took the scenic route, showing Jessie roads and countryside views she'd never seen before, even in almost five years of living in the area. She couldn't take any of it in. She couldn't shake the feeling the guest book had given her. Surely Molly hadn't lied about her alibi?

The big houses came into view, pushing Jessie to the front of the bus. She hopped off and ran into the cul-de-sac and didn't stop until she was at Molly's door. All the lights were off. Not a great start.

"Molly, are you in?" she called through the frosted glass when there was no response. "It's Jessie. I have some news about the case."

Jessie didn't have any news, but given how often Molly had been asking Barker for updates, she had to believe the promise would bring Molly to the door. Like Molly had done before, Jessie crouched and poked a finger against the spring-loaded letterbox. She looked down the hall to the kitchen, where a table was piled high with letters.

The table was in the same place as Walter's.

The exact same place.

And it wasn't the only thing precisely the same. Jessie pulled away from the letterbox and looked around the cul-de-sac. All the houses were identical in size and shape. Only their windows, doors, and gardens were different.

Jessie crossed the cul-de-sac and pushed in Walter's letterbox. The table, where they'd found Walter slumped in his dinner was in the kitchen at the end of the hall, through an archway with no door. But Jessie already knew she'd be able to see straight down to the kitchen. She'd looked down the same hall when DI Moyes had come out for her hot chocolate.

Just as Molly had done on the night they'd found Walter.

And somehow, even as she must have been staring at her father's body, Molly hadn't flinched.

16

The woman next to Jessie on the packed bus was staring right at her. She tried to stop her knee from bouncing, but the nervous energy only transferred to her teeth chewing at her lip. Phone at her ear, she willed the bus to speed up in the Saturday traffic. Far off in the countryside, the sun was gliding toward the horizon.

"*Come on!*" Jessie urged, loud enough that the silent passengers joined her neighbour in staring.

Damn Father David for telling everyone to put their phones on silent during the ceremony. How could nobody be picking up when she knew who was behind everything? Calling the police on the bus would attract more than stares, but what if someone else was in danger?

Jessie remembered Molly's plea in the basement.

"Both of my parents have been murdered," she had said with the straightest of faces. "Do you think there's a chance that I'm next?"

What a snake.

"Can someone answer their phone?" Jessie muttered as the call rang out. "Anyone?"

"...and then the horse ran through the tent," Roxy said, and the crowd in the village hall chuckled in their seats. "And the tent fell onto the fire. You should have seen Leah. As cool as a cucumber, she plucked this flaming polyester tent from the fire and stomped it out like it was nothing. Turned out her school homework was in there. You should have seen the size of this horse."

Roxy raised her champagne glass to indicate the animal's height. Julia was sure it had been a pony, but the crowd were lapping it up. Leah's nervous expression was easing the more Roxy talked, and Johnny had been laughing the whole time. Julia was glad she hadn't put up a fight when the decision about who would give the speech came up.

"This giant chestnut horse on the run from the riding centre reared on its back two legs," Roxy continued, "and there's Leah, too busy blowing out the burning pages of her exercise books to notice. And out of nowhere, Johnny, who wouldn't have said boo to a goose, charged in, the hero of the hour. He dragged her out of the way seconds before the horse stomped down exactly where she'd been. That swiftly ended Leah's horse phase. But, more than anything, we should have known right then and there that these two were destined to be with each other. Of course, they had to take the long way around." Roxy grinned at them as she toasted her glass. "In all seriousness, I couldn't be happier that two of my best friends, who I've been lucky enough to know my whole life, have found love in each other. And I promise this isn't one of those 'we'll marry each other if we're single when we're forty' pacts. Johnny and I made one of those when we were nineteen, and I can't think of a more perfect person to give up my back-pocket husband for. Leah, Johnny, *wherever* your lives take you together." She paused. For the first time during the speech, it looked like she might cry. "I have no doubt you're going to have all the happiness in the world if you remember to follow this essential piece of advice. Please stay away from horses." The room chortled. "But most importantly, be kind to each other. That's all you need. Since you were both always such massive teacher's pets, take that as an order from Miss

Carter. Join me in raising a glass to the new Mr and Mrs Watson."

Julia lifted her glass along with the rest of the room. Roxy sat down to applause, and Julia gave her friend's knee a supportive squeeze under the table. The newlyweds were both dabbing at the corners of their eyes.

"Well done. That'll be a tough one to follow," Julia whispered, looking out at the room of smiling faces. There was a seat empty next to Dot and Percy. "Have you seen Jessie?"

"Not since the church."

Roxy's speech was impossible to follow. Johnny's best man was a young journalist from the newspaper whose voice was shaking as much as the hands clutching his written speech. He struggled through a story of Johnny ordering too many paperclips, which was the set-up and punchline. He sank into his seat to tepid slow claps, ending the speeches.

"The bride and groom are going to take an hour to freshen up," the DJ announced over the sound system as Leah's crew rushed in to start moving the tables away from the dancefloor. "Kids disco starts in ten minutes. Who's ready to get this party started?"

Pushing through the crowd as they congregated at the bar near the back – a pop-up of Richie's – Julia followed her gran's giant red hat as it bobbed in the direction of the door.

"Have you seen Jessie?"

"Not since the church," Dot said, in too much of a hurry to stop. "She missed the whole meal. Delicious crème brûlée, by the way. I'll keep an eye out for her."

"Where are you rushing off to?" Julia hurried to keep up as they reached the green. "Can I hear a walkie-talkie crackling in your bag?"

"No." Dot switched her bag to her opposite arm. "Maybe? Percy said he'd just heard something interesting on the..."

"On what?"

"On the radio."

"I'm guessing it wasn't a catchy new pop song?" Julia grabbed her gran's arm to stop her fleeing. "Or a *regular* radio. Gran, you said you didn't buy a police radio."

"First of all, that's what you *told* me to say. 'Please tell me you don't have a police radio'. Since you were so awfully polite, I was simply following your instruction. And secondly, I didn't *buy* it. I found it."

"Did you walk into the station and rip it from the wall?"

"Don't be silly," Dot said, pushing open her gate. "I fished it from their skip. I'm not a total barbarian,

Julia. It's recycling. Really, I can only watch so much *Countdown*. I need to know what's going on *here*. Did you know Betty and Patricia are battling over a strip of grass between their properties? They call the police on each other every time one of them dares cut it."

"I'm guessing you're not rushing back for a grass update?"

"Percy popped home to check on the dogs during that poor boy's speech. Honestly, someone should buy him a razor for Christmas. He had more beard on his neck than his face." Dot burst through the front door and headed straight down the hall. "Percy, what's the emergency?"

Julia followed her gran into the dining room, once the hub for the neighbourhood watch. The chalkboard was still on the wall – another of Dot's scavenged items – but family pictures had replaced the maps of the village and operations schedules. Percy was hunched at a large console full of flashing lights and buttons on the writing desk, listening through clunky headphones. The dogs were wandering around in the back garden.

"What is it, Percy?"

"They're still speaking in codes," he said, squinting, with one headphone pressed at his ear, "but oh boy, things are heating up. It's been quite the day. They kept talking about wool earlier."

"Wool?" Julia echoed.

"Might have been code for something. It really is hard to decipher what they're saying. But for the last five minutes, they've been talking about mobilising units. It's all very frantic. I think they're going to make an arrest."

"About time!" Dot leaned in and pressed her ear to the headphones. "What are they saying now?"

"Hang on, love," he said, twisting one of the dials. "'She's at the school. I repeat, she's at the school.'"

"Who's at the school?" Dot demanded, squeezing herself onto the stool. "Let me listen."

"They're not being specific," he said, resisting Dot's attempt to take off the headphones. "I'm afraid this isn't a telephone. I can't just ask."

Julia left them to squabble as her mind connected, or rather, knitted, the threads together. Back at the village hall, Barker and Roxy were lingering by the door.

"Play's just about to start," Roxy said, teeth chattering as she checked her watch. "Think we have time to pop over and show our faces before Mr and Mrs Watson get back?"

"I insist we do." Julia strained her ear for sirens, but none were in the air yet. "I think it's going to be quite the show."

Jessie hopped off the bus near Fern Moore and, waving her phone in the air, flagged down the taxi she'd booked. It would get her to Peridale twelve minutes quicker than the rest of the bus journey, and she needed every minute she could get.

Nobody was picking up their phone.

Nobody except for Julia's sister, Sue.

"Oh, thank you!" Jessie cried down the phone as she jumped into the backseat of the taxi. "*Sue*? Is Julia there? It's an emergency. It's about the murders."

"Hello?" a small voice mumbled down the phone as PSY's 'Gangnam Style' blasted in the background. "*Hellooo*?"

"Who is this?"

"Pearl."

How was Jessie on the phone with her three-year-old cousin?

"Pearl, sweetie, can you find your mummy and put her on the phone? It's Jessie."

There was a splash, and 'Gangnam Style' gurgled into the 'Cha Cha Slide'.

"Am I in a glass?" Jessie called down the phone. "Pearl, did you put mummy's phone in a *drink*?"

The call cut out.

What was happening?

"St. Peter's School in Peridale," Jessie said to the taxi driver. "It's an emergency."

The taxi pulled away from the side of the road and joined the flow of traffic behind the bus Jessie had just jumped off. Holding in a scream, Jessie tried to call Julia again.

17

$\mathcal{T}$hey passed through the gates, and Roxy jogged ahead, leaving Julia to fill Barker in on her theory as they hurried across the playground to the sound of tepid applause.

"But Molly *hired* me," Barker whispered as they swished through the leaves. "That makes no sense. Why would she do that if she'd killed her parents?"

"Remember what you said about Walter when you considered him? He'd need to be clever to fool a PI," Julia said. "If I'm right, Molly's got away with this for thirty years. Why would she worry about getting caught now, after she covered her tracks so well with all her staging at the cul-de-sac. Still, she's leaving tracks whether she knows it. She visited the charity shop on Monday morning. She told Libbie she was there to talk about the funeral, to bury the hatchet."

"And to steal the knife and beads," Barker said, holding open the door. "It takes an incredibly cold and calculated person to return to a crime scene and swap out a knife. She left her father for dead twice. She's been playing the grieving daughter right under our noses. How was she so convincing?"

"It's a role she's been playing for three decades," Julia replied, lowering her voice as they crossed the dark reception area toward the parents standing at the back of the assembly hall. "Can you see her?"

Julia tiptoed over the crowd of parents recording their children during the *Alice in Wonderland* tea party scene. The Mad Hatter was giving a monologue, his unsure delivery making Julia dread all the plays she would have to sit through if Olivia chose that path.

"Nothing worse than kids trying to act," Barker whispered, reading her mind. A couple of parents glared, and one woman shushed him with a finger at her lips. They stepped back, and he said, "I can't see her. Can you?"

"No, but you've been spotted."

Barker turned as Daphne marched up to him, clearly ready to spit fire.

"What are *you* doing here?" she whispered

aggressively. "You're not going to ruin this for Kyle Junior. He's worked hard learning his lines. When are you going to leave me alone?"

"We're not here to see you."

Alice was ready to leave the tea party, and two more parents shushed them.

"Have you seen Molly?" Julia asked.

"Who?"

"Miss Harkup?"

"Oh, the cardigan woman I used to work with." She nodded in the direction of the corridor heading toward the upper years. "She was feeding the kids their lines, but she ran off. You're not the first to turn up to try and ruin the play. That chick who got arrested demanded to see her right as Alice was drinking the shrinking potion."

"Libbie's here?"

Julia set off down the corridor, past the library and canteen, and through the doors to the upper area. The Year Six classroom was in the same room. As she approached the door, and she saw Molly through the glass. Julia pushed the door open, and the teacher whipped away from staring into the dark countryside.

"Julia," she said, pushing forward a smile. "You made it. I was just having a moment. Everything's got a little much for me. Pushed myself too hard."

"You're bleeding," Julia pointed out. "Looks like you've been in a scuffle."

Molly's fingers went up to the blood on her forehead, and when she pulled them down, she stared for a moment. Julia could hear the story being written in the silence.

"It was Libbie," Molly said, wiping at the blood with the sleeve of her cardigan. "She turned up here and attacked me. I still think she did it, Julia. I think she faked her alibi somehow. She's unhinged. She's always been this way."

Julia groaned. She'd believed Molly's version of Libbie since their first conversation. She'd been convincing then, just as she'd been every time Molly pushed them in her cousin's direction. Her insistence of Libbie's guilt should have been a sign. What was it she'd accused Libbie of? Always twisting things to suit her.

"You're good," Julia said. "I'll give you that. But you have kept up this charade up since 1989, so I'm not surprised."

"Excuse me?" Molly kept her cool. "I don't know what you're talking about."

Julia narrowed her eyes at the teacher. Had she pulled at the wrong thread? She thought back to that timeline stuck to the board in Barker's office. She'd always been sure she'd been missing something, but the clues were there.

"The champagne," Julia said. "You took the methanol from the car factory where you worked, and then over lunch, you fed it to her through the champagne."

"This has gone quite far—"

"Then you came back to school to find her," Julia continued, "but you didn't know Daphne had seen you on her way out. Not that she ever thought to put the pieces together, but why would she? You were just someone she served in the canteen at the car factory. She didn't know you were Molly's daughter. You put your mother in that box, dug a hole – a grave – and left her there. How could you do that to your own mother, Molly?"

Molly's calm stare deadened, and quick as a flash, she picked up one of the tiny chairs and launched it across the classroom. Julia dove out of the way, winding herself against a table in the process. Molly sprinted for the door, and Julia's fingers grazed her cardigan as she passed. The door ripped open and swung back in its frame, and Molly was gone.

Julia staggered forward, catching her breath as the tight sensation in her midsection faded. She straightened and made for the door, but a grunt made her turn around. A hand clung to the side of the desk.

Libbie stared up at her with weary eyes, a pair of scissors jutting from her stomach.

"You're right," Libbie struggled for breath. "She ... she framed me. Twice. I ... I knew it had to be her."

"Don't try to talk."

"Monday," Libbie coughed. "The knife. The bracelet."

The door opened and Roxy and Barker rushed in.

"What the—" Roxy cried. "I'll call an ambulance. Where's Molly?"

"She's made a run for it."

"She thinks she's going to get away with this?" Barker asked, crouching at Libbie's side. "Did she confess?"

"As good as," Julia said, glancing at the chair. "Molly was waiting for Libbie to bleed to death while talking to me like nothing had happened. She didn't so much as glance at the desk. Who is this—"

The lights cut out, and the terrified screams of children echoed down the hall. Libbie's hand limply wrapped around Julia's.

"Stay with us, Libbie," Julia whispered. "Roxy? How long on the paramedics?"

"They're almost here."

"Barker, keep Libbie talking," she ordered, kissing him as she let her hand slip away from Libbie's.

"Molly can't get away with this. Roxy, where's the fuse box?"

"This way."

Julia took one last glance at Libbie, grumbling on the floor with the scissors poking from her stomach, as ambulance sirens grew closer. Children's scissors were as small as their chairs.

She'd make it.

She had to.

Julia and Roxy hurried back toward the assembly hall as a stampede of phone flashlights lit up the entrance hallway like reflections from a scattered disco ball. Julia sniffed, picking up on the smoke that was making the crowd of panicked costumed children and parents run for the front door. Julia and Roxy darted into the clearing assembly hall. The last of the children rushed away as flames engulfed the painted set.

"It's spreading up the stage curtains!" Roxy cried, lunging for a red fire extinguisher by the piano. "Julia, there's another extinguisher in the gym cupboard. We need to stop this."

But Julia's eyes were already on the swinging double doors in the corner of the room. The blaze burned against her cheeks as she ran toward them. She burst out into the cold night, the wind dragging at her chiffon dress and bouncy hair. Dark countryside spread out before her in every direction. Molly could have gone anywhere.

"Julia?"

She turned back and grabbed the extinguisher from the gym cupboard, glad to see paramedics rushing through the stragglers.

"Molly swung big with her getaway distraction," Roxy called as they sprayed the thick foam on the flames.

"And it worked."

"I don't understand why Molly killed her parents."

"Thirty years apart, they figured out that she took the charity money."

"But why did she need it?"

"Only Molly can tell us that," Julia said as the last of the foam left her extinguisher. "If she gets away, we might never find out."

"Fire's out, and it looks like the police are outside. They need to know that Mad Molly is on the loose. I can't believe I pretended to have a good time at her Christmas parties every year. How can someone so boring and polite be so ruthless?"

"Boring and polite sounds like the perfect cover to me."

The paramedics rushed down the hallway with Libbie on a stretcher. Julia and Roxy followed them out. Three police cars and an ambulance were parked on the playground, and groups of children and adults hung around, watching the scene unfold. The paramedics carried Libbie into the back of the ambulance and drove off with the siren blaring.

"How is it that *you're* here?" DI Moyes cried, walking from her car. "Even with a wedding to attend, you still find the time."

"Are you here for Molly?"

"As it happens, yes. Those fibres were wool. They matched a cardigan she still owns. What's happened? We were hoping to catch her at the end of the play."

"She set fire to the set and legged it," Roxy said. "I wasted so many hours helping her paint that thing yesterday. If I'd known she cared so little, I wouldn't have tried so hard to stay in the lines. Julia, isn't that Jessie?"

Julia squinted into the crowd as they parted by the gates. Jessie emerged next to Amir, who was pushing a wheelbarrow. In that wheelbarrow, Molly was bound and gagged with rope. When he reached the middle of the parked cars, Amir dumped her out onto the leaves, and she rolled onto her side. Julia felt his rage as he slammed the barrow down next to her, causing her to flinch. Julia couldn't blame him one bit.

"Don't any of you check your phones?" Jessie cried. "I don't know how many times I called you before giving up. Amir answered on the *first* attempt.

He was supposed to get to the school before me to tell you all I found out about Molly, but he got stuck in the same traffic jam as my bus and my taxi." Jessie took a calming breath. "It all worked out for the best because we met at the lane just as Molly was making a run for it. How do you like our citizen's arrest?"

"You got the job done," DI Moyes said, clicking the uniformed officers over. "Given how slippery she's been, I don't trust her not to pull a Houdini and wriggle free."

"Before you take her away, I need to know why," Julia said, squatting to Molly's level as the officers cranked metal cuffs around her wrists. "You painted a rosy picture of your relationship with your mother, but since you were the only one, I guess it was far from it. She told Libbie about her proposal, but not her own daughter?"

Molly forced the rope out of her mouth and let it fall against her heaving collarbones as she fought for breath. She turned her eyes toward the school.

"I loved my mother and father very dearly," Molly said, which caused more than a few snorts of laughter and gasps of disbelief. "It's true. I idolised them. When I was a young girl, I wanted for nothing. They gave me all the love and attention a child could need. I wanted to be a teacher just like them. Why wouldn't I want to be like my favourite people?" Molly's smile soured. "Maybe if they hadn't tried so hard when I was so young, I wouldn't have been so aware of the way things changed. They were both desperate to prove themselves at school, especially my mother. She offered to run every club, direct every production, and raise money for every charity she heard about. How much attention do you think they had for smart, sensible Molly at home? My mother cared more about everyone else's children rather than her own."

"It must have stung when Libbie turned up," Julia said.

"*Stung*?" Molly choked on the word. "It *ruined* my life. As if things weren't bad enough with two parents who were never home, Libbie showed up and turned everything upside down. My mum latched onto her straight away. Forgave her for everything she ever did. I'd spent years trying to please my mother, trying to get her to notice that I needed her love too. Do you know how many hours I spent helping her mark her mountains of homework when she was too busy with everything else? Or how I came here on my weekends to make her displays because she could never find the time? Funnily enough, she found time whenever *Libbie* needed her for something. Predictable, steady Molly was never quite damaged enough to deserve fixing. I knew if I was going to stand a chance of getting my parents back, I had to get Libbie out of the way."

"So, you took the charity money and framed Libbie just to get her out of the picture?" Barker asked.

"Make no mistake, I needed that money more than any of them." Molly struggled into a sitting position. "Libbie messed up constantly and got everything handed to her. I was working myself into the ground with two jobs, and I could barely make ends meet. I tried fixing things with credit cards, but that made it all worse."

"That off-handed comment you made," Roxy said with a gasp. "When I knocked over your junk mail. You said you wouldn't get another credit card."

"But that's not true," Barker added. "You tried to pay for my time with a credit card."

"Old habits die hard." Molly shrugged. "I'm much better at paying it off these days, but back then, I was always months behind. The amount my mum raised for that children's hospital ... it was exactly what I needed to wipe the slate clean. It would kill two birds with one stone."

"You put the money box in Libbie's bag," Julia said.

"She went down to Woolworths to steal cassette

tapes every Saturday like clockwork. My mum believed her when she said she bought them, but she never had any receipts and always had money to waste on sweets. I knew a busted safe box in the bottom of her bag would finally get them to call the police, so I followed her. When I saw the cassettes go into her bag, I pointed her out to the manager and left. He did the rest for me. It couldn't have worked better."

"Only, it didn't work," Julia said. "You took it a step further and murdered your mother. She must have found out."

"The night before the play, she visited Libbie to try and resolve things. She called and told me she thought Libbie was innocent. She asked to meet for lunch."

"And you just happened to have methanol on you?" Jessie asked.

"I saw the effects of methanol poisoning at work. Someone drank some as a bet when a guy told him it was 'pure alcohol', but I don't think he expected to end up in the hospital. People said he was lucky not to have died, so I took a bottle."

"You took methanol to a lunch with your mother to poison her?" Amir growled. "You're a monster."

"That's not what happened." Molly turned to glare at him. "I took the methanol to lunch with my mother because I planned to find out what Libbie had said. I was going to poison Libbie."

"So much better," Roxy said sarcastically. "Murdering a fifteen year old to keep your theft a secret seems reasonable."

"If I could make it look like a suicide, she'd die with everyone thinking she took the money. It would put me in the clear." Molly searched the crowd as though looking for support. "It was supposed to fix my life. I could use the money to pay off my debts. Then I could rebuild my relationship with my mum."

"But Felicity accused you?" Barker asked. "She must have."

Molly nodded. "She had no proof, but my dad told her about finding my credit card letters, and she just had a feeling. Maybe I denied it too hard. I knew where she'd kept the money, and I had access to Libbie's backpack. It was only a matter of time before she found out."

"So you poisoned her," Julia said, barely able to believe what she was hearing. "You sent your mother off to a slow and painful death for a few thousand pounds?"

"I didn't *mean* to," Molly said, searching again. "It was an accident. Well, not an accident, but a moment of insanity. I wanted to be a teacher. How could I let it get out? She was nervous about the play, so she kept sipping her champagne. She didn't notice that I kept topping it up with methanol, so I kept doing it. I regretted it immediately."

"Did you tell her she'd been poisoned?" Amir asked bluntly. "Did you call medical professionals?"

"No."

"Then you didn't regret it!" Amir roared. Jessie rested her hand on his shoulder. "You talk and talk, but none of it means anything. The picture you've painted of Flick, of my Flick, is wrong. It's so cynical. She was a kind, gracious, charitable woman, and you sound like a jealous, whiny child who couldn't stand that she wasn't always the centre of attention."

"Says the guy she rejected," Molly said with a smirk. "When I came to the school, I found her body in the bathroom stall. I couldn't believe how quickly it had worked. She was beyond help, so I locked myself in the next stall. I waited until the police cleared off after that smashed window, and then I improvised. I'd made a mistake, but I couldn't change it, so what was the point of both of us suffering?" Molly staggered to her feet, and everyone except for DI Moyes and the officers stepped back. "I tried to put some of it right, didn't I? After I had my mother's handwriting convincing enough, I went up to Scotland to show my face to her sister and the rest of my cousins. Asked if they'd seen her and posted the letters. I got Libbie out of prison, didn't I? I could have let her rot."

"But you tarnished Flick's name in the process," Amir cried. "Don't you hear yourself?"

"I continued what my mum started here. I'm a good teacher, aren't I, Roxy?" She lunged forward, and the officers yanked her back. "Tell them I'm as good as Flick. Tell them!"

"You don't deserve to speak her name." Amir spat at the ground. "You stole her from the kids she taught and from every child who didn't get the chance. You took her from me."

"But all my years here, they matter." Molly's lips blubbered as she looked at the school. "I tried to put things right. They matter."

"Molly, you murdered your father over the weekend," Julia reminded her. "You repeated your mistake from 1989. You didn't learn from it."

"Stubborn old fool," Molly muttered. "Just like my mother, he realised it could only have been me. I denied it, and then I left him to his dinner."

"And snuck in through the back door using his key to stab him in the back?" Jessie said, shaking her head. "All while trying to frame your cousin again. Nice guestbook trick, by the way. You're bonkers, lady."

"If only I'd paid more attention during the bathroom planning meetings." Molly hunched her shoulders and started laughing. "I might have got away with it for another thirty years."

"I think we've heard enough." DI Moyes clicked her fingers, and the officers grabbed her arms. "Molly Harkup, you're under arrest for the murders of Felicity Campbell and Walter Harkup."

With tears swelling along her lashes, Molly smiled at the building as the officers pulled her away.

"Tell the kids I'm sorry, Miss Carter," Molly called. "Please?"

Roxy couldn't seem to bring herself to look at her colleague as she desperately tried to turn back the whole way to the gates. Julia wrapped her hand around her friend's.

"It's actually over," Roxy said, struggled out a sigh of relief. "All these years later, we finally know the truth. Well, almost the whole truth. I should have asked if she saw her dad take my cinnamon roll in the staffroom."

"I'm glad we can finally lay Flick to rest," Amir muttered as he turned away. "But I wish I hadn't spent all these years being civil to the person who took her from this world. I'll never forgive myself for not seeing through her act."

Amir followed behind DI Moyes as officers pushed Molly into the back of a police car. Beyond them, the wedding reception was in full swing in the softly lit village hall.

"What now?" Jessie asked.

"They're going to want us to give statements about everything that happened here tonight," Barker said.

"Statements can wait." Julia looped her arm through Roxy's and set off through the leaves. "We have a wedding to get back to."

18

a crowd had gathered outside the village hall to watch the ambulance and police cars drive by. Johnny and Leah were among them, holding each other with the world's worries etched on their faces.

"What's going on?" Dot asked. "Children and parents ran away like the place was on fire."

"It was, briefly," Julia said, patting Roxy on the shoulder. "Miss Carter took care of it."

"And the police cars?" Percy asked. "There were quite a few."

"They took care of Molly," Barker said.

"It's over, Gran."

"*Molly*?" Dot gasped. "Molly murdered her

parents? There was always something strange about her. I *knew* it was her from the beginning."

"Sure you did," Jessie said, forging ahead toward the village hall, looping her arm through Dot's. "If Evelyn ever goes blind in her third eye, you can step in to meet the village's psychic needs. You've been so spot-on lately. Only took you three guesses."

Julia followed behind, glad to give Johnny and Leah the good news that the case was now closed.

"Then I'd say that's cause for celebration," Johnny said, holding the door open for them. "We didn't want to cut the cake without you. I can't believe how cool it looks, Julia."

"I can," Leah said. "I never doubted it would be anything less than absolute perfection."

Julia was glad someone hadn't.

"To Julia," DI Moyes raised her champagne glass to Julia as she joined her at the buffet. "The vigilante baker. Though, for the record, we'd figured it out, and we've been gathering the evidence."

"Well done."

"She really pulled the wool over our eyes, no pun intended. If she's lucky, she'll end up in a prison that gives the inmates access to knitting needles, though after what she did to her father, I'm not sure I'd trust her with anything sharp for a while." Champagne glass held to her face, Moyes smiled as she looked across the dancefloor. Julia followed her gaze to Roxy, dancing with Olivia who was wide awake despite bedtime having passed an hour ago. "Your redheaded friend?"

"Roxy."

"Roxy." Moyes' husky tone gave the name more seriousness than Roxy had ever displayed. "Is she single?"

"She is."

"Interesting." The DI reached into her pocket and pulled out a card. "Will you give her my number? I'm afraid I have a weak spot for feisty redheads."

"You don't strike me as the shy type, Detective," Julia said, nudging her forward with her shoulder. "Why don't you go and give it to her yourself, DI Moyes?"

"Really?" She tossed the champagne back before slamming the glass on the buffet table. "And please, just Laura. You're all awfully polite around here. Makes me feel like I'm always at tea with my dreadfully posh aunt."

Laura Moyes tugged at her blazer and checked her breath on her hand as she approached Roxy, who'd already handed Olivia over to Sue for a waltz. Laura doubled back when she reached Roxy and immediately turned and stepped into Roxy's view. They talked a little before Laura handed over her card, and Roxy looked confused until Laura leaned to her ear.

"Oh," Julia saw Roxy mouth. "*Oh.*"

The lights dimmed, and a spotlight appeared in the darkened room. As though from nowhere, fluffy white cloud of dry ice floated across the starlit dancefloor.

"Ladies and gentlemen," the DJ said smoothly from his booth, "if you'll please clear the dancefloor, we'd like to welcome the bride and groom for their first dance."

Propped at the bar, with the smoke lapping at her feet, Jessie scrolled through the admission form on her phone. She ticked the last few confirmation boxes and rewarded herself with a sip of her espresso martini. Richie made a decent cocktail, but she'd had better in a bar in Berlin. She scrolled to the bottom of the page until nothing was left to do. She hit submit and placed the phone screen down on the bar.

"That's never a good sign," Barker said as he pulled up a chair next to her. He motioned to Richie, who was busy on the side of the bar dazzling Dot and Percy with his cocktail tricks. "Boy trouble?"

"Do you know me at all?"

"Of course. You're my spitting image, remember?"

"It's not boy trouble," she said. "I just applied to college."

"Seriously?"

"Seriously."

"Jessie, that's amazing news." The smile across his face surprised her, and her insides warmed up. "I'm so proud of you. I knew you had it in you. Journalism?"

"I have some unfinished business to attend to before then," she said. "Truth is, I haven't decided what I want to do. Who I want to be. Thought I'd figure that out travelling, but I was having too much fun living to think too far ahead. But now that I'm home, I need something new. I need the right foundation. It's a short course that will help me get my high school GCSEs. Maths, English, and science, but it's a start."

"All the others are fluff anyway," he whispered, giving her a hug. "Really, I'm so proud of you. Have you told your mum yet?"

"You're the first."

"Then I'm honoured."

Barker ordered a matching espresso martini, and he raised a toast to her. Their glasses clinked, and they spun around in their chairs to watch the wedding. Johnny and Leah couldn't have looked more perfect for each other as they floated through the clouds to Michael Bublé crooning 'The Best Is Yet To Come'.

"Almost makes you want to throw up," Jessie said after a sip, though she couldn't help but smile; they did look rather adorable together. "And anyway, I'm not the only one with unfinished business. Are we going to talk about what DI Moyes said to you?"

"About?"

"Don't play dumb. Your old job at the station? She stunned you into silence with it."

"Let's just say it gave me a lot to think about."

"Are you going for it? Being a PI isn't exactly lighting your world on fire."

"It's steady and flexible," he said, swirling the coffee beans around in his drink. "But you're right. It's not lighting my world on fire. Neither is the idea of being a detective again. Not right now, at least. But you might be onto something. I think I do have some unfinished business. How does *The Body in the Time Capsule* sound?"

"For what?"

"Barker Brown's long-awaited second novel." He slid off the stool and waved to Julia, who'd finished dancing with Roxy. "Who knows."

Barker joined Julia for a dance as other couples

floated away on the clouds, leaving Jessie at the bar. She wasn't much of a dancer. She picked up her phone, and refreshed the application. Pending. It wasn't a rejection yet. She couldn't believe Barker had thought she was having boy trouble.

Scrolling through her contacts, she stopped at a name she hadn't used for a while. Billy Matthews. If not for Daphne bringing him up, Jessie might not have thought about him, but she was at a wedding, drinking martinis.

When else was she going to drunk call her ex-boyfriend?

"I'm sorry," a robotic voice gurgled down the line, *"the number you are trying to call has been disconnected."*

Probably for the best.

She rechecked the college application.

Future pending.

By midnight, only the four friends remained. They were huddled around an electric firepit behind the village hall, roasting marshmallows on metal skewers. Leah's final planned event for the evening. They talked about the case, they talked about the wedding, and when a silence built up, for once, it wasn't comfortable. Julia had sensed what was coming when they'd headed outside to leave the cleaning crew to start putting the village hall back together in time for the following day's slimming club meeting.

"Johnny and I, we have something to tell you," Leah said, looking up at her new husband, her head on his chest. "Johnny's been offered a job up north, and..." Her voice wobbled. "I can't tell them, Johnny, you do it."

"I've accepted," he said, his smile as nervous as Leah's. "You're looking at the new editor of all news for Sphere Media. I'm about to get a giant office with a window, my own team, and actual resources so that the things I'm working on can be seen by more than the few people who still pick up the paper around here." He paused to peel off a layer of his marshmallow, but it didn't make it to his mouth. "And it means we're going to be moving."

"Totally shocking news," Roxy exclaimed.

"Completely surprised," Julia added.

Leah looked between them before sitting upright.

"Johnny, we said we weren't going to tell them until after the wedding."

"It slipped out. I was dying to tell someone."

"And how great were we for not bringing it up?" Roxy nudged Leah in the ribs. "It's given us some time to adjust to the idea. We'll all have to adapt. Cars are a thing. And trains. And everything's online now anyway."

"I know," Leah said, smiling through tears. "I've loved my few years back in the village, but it's time to move on. To see what else is out there. I can plan weddings anywhere. New challenges await us. And it's not happening right away." Leah dabbed delicately at her cheeks, and her makeup was still intact. "The house needs to sell first, and Johnny's agreed to a transition period at *The Peridale Post*."

"They're letting me train up my replacement. Part of me only agreed so the place wouldn't go up in flames without me. I wouldn't have got this opportunity if the paper hadn't given me my first chance. I went from making cups of tea to editing the paper, and I'll be forever grateful for that. And as tough as it's been watching cutbacks empty out the office around me, I'm proud that I could keep the ship steady. Time for someone else to give it a go. And who knows, I might be totally rubbish at my new job and be back in six months."

"Worry about that another night." Roxy left the firepit and tugged open the doors. "Here and now, we're all together, and you two just got married. *And* a murderer is behind bars. I'd say it's time to celebrate. Shots at the bar."

"Do we have to?" Leah groaned.

"Yes," the other three replied as one.

Walking home with Roxy more than a little tipsy Julia was glad they had each other for support. She wasn't sure who was holding who up.

"I'll be out of your hair tomorrow," Roxy said, trying her best not to slur. "Maybe the day after. I've overstayed my welcome."

"That sofa is yours *any* time." Julia's voice sounded the same as Roxy's. "I mean it. Leave me out of the loop again, and I'll—"

"Stick me in a time capsule?" Roxy gasped at her own joke. "That was naughty."

Julia stifled her laugh. "Bad Roxy."

"Rest in peace Miss Campbell," Roxy whispered. "And Walter, too, I guess. You miserable old swine."

They staggered past Leah and Johnny's house – the newlyweds had left before Roxy dragged Julia into Richie's.

"I know they haven't left yet, but do you think they'll ever come back?" Roxy asked, fiddling with the garden gate to Julia's cottage. "One day, when we're all ancient and going crazy in the old folks home?"

"My gran would somehow still be alive."

"A floating head in a jar."

They reached Julia's front door, and, after a few stabs, the key entered the lock. Turning back to look across the lane as the lights went out in Leah and Johnny's bedroom window, Julia said, "I hope so. Peridale has a way of bringing people back together."

"Like us." Roxy rested her head on Julia's shoulder. "And then there were two."

19

Two weeks later, while Johnny and Leah were on their honeymoon in the Maldives, Julia and Roxy watched the new time capsule's burial. Even with the drizzle, they weren't the only ones to watch the new tube go into the ground. Libbie was amongst the dozens who'd turned up for the occasion, though she was still using crutches after her near miss with a pair of children's scissors.

To spare the capsule being dug up again if the records ever went missing – though it was now assumed Molly had been behind the lack of records – the governors had coughed up the money to create a specially built stone tunnel.

Along with the items that had been buried in 1990,

the current students had added new contributions. The governors had also invited any pupils who'd been at the school during the first burial to add new pieces. Julia had considered writing a second volume of her handwritten recipe book. After taking some pictures, she'd been happy to let the original go back into the ground.

Instead, she'd worked with her three closest friends to compile a record detailing the life and death of Felicity Campbell. They'd been as honest as they could, including newspaper articles and police photographs to paint a complete picture of the circumstances surrounding her death, but most of the book focused on her life.

They told stories of the charitable, kind, patient teacher who'd always cast them in plays, spared them from embarrassment, or helped with a stutter. The teacher they'd loved to bake for. The teacher they just plain loved. Thanks to Roxy schooling most of their children, they'd been able to get the book into enough hands of former pupils to fill it with happy stories. Even Amir had added a page about their writing lessons, though he'd left out the detail of his proposal.

"In memory of Felicity Campbell," the governor said as she sealed the new monument under a shiny plaque, "and Walter Harkup. We bury this capsule underground so that future generations can discover the story of our past and present-day lives here at St. Peter's in Peridale."

There were sniffles all around as the rain fell, but Julia mostly felt the joy in the air. They'd set Miss Campbell's legacy straight, and now she could finally rest with the truth out there for all – including future generations – to see.

"How's he been?" Julia asked, nodding at Amir. The groundskeeper was raking leaves on the grass as they followed the flow of adults across the playground.

"I think he's found his peace," Roxy said with a wave. He returned it with a nod. "I asked if he would put the ring back in, but he said he wanted to keep it this time. Helping him feel close to Flick. I think that's sweet."

"I think that's sweet too."

"Felicity was so many things to different people," Roxy said, holding open the gate for Julia. "I still don't know which version of her is real."

"What if they all are? She was the teacher we loved, the mother Libbie never had. She was the woman Walter and Amir both fell in love with at different times for different reasons. She was also the mother who made Molly feel overlooked and the authority who cast Kyle Nation out of school."

"Teachers still talk about him in whispers like he's

the gold standard for tearaway children," Roxy said, whispering. "The ones who remembered him were dreading teaching Kyle Junior, but he's a sweetheart. And he's being half-raised by Daphne, so she must be doing something right these days. As for me, I'll remember Miss Campbell as the best headteacher this school never had. Speaking of which—"

"You haven't!" Julia stopped. "Oh, Rox. Congratulations, I'm so—"

"You're right, I haven't," Roxy cut in, nudging Julia's shoulder. "They thought it was best to go with someone with more experience to 'steady the ship during these hard times blah blah blah', but you know what, they're right. I wanted a new challenge, but I don't think I'm *quite* ready for that job just yet."

"I'm sure a challenge will come along soon."

"It already has." Roxy bit into her lip, and in the hesitation, Julia prepared herself for the final piece of her friend group to fall away. "I'm moving on up in the world to Year Six. They offered me the job this morning. Miss Carter is about to get a new classroom *and* a pay rise."

The Liverpool school advert had never come up.

"So, you're sticking around then?" Julia asked.

"You can't get rid of me that easy." She looked back at the school. "Besides, this place needs someone with their head screwed on to look out for it. I'm not entirely convinced some of my fellow teachers aren't hiding a murder or two up their sleeves."

"Then back to the café to celebrate. The cake is on me."

"No can do, my friend," Roxy said as they came to the end of the lane. "I have a date to get to."

Julia concealed her smile. They hadn't talked about DI Moyes, either. "Anyone who I know?"

"Let's just say you're not the only one who can bag yourself a DI." Roxy kissed Julia goodbye and hurried off with a spring in her step. "Wish me luck."

"You don't need it. Just be yourself."

"And here I thought you were good at giving advice."

Leaving Roxy to go to Richie's, Julia returned to the café. At the table nearest the counter, Barker bounced Olivia on his knee. The 'I'M ONE TODAY!' pink badge pinned to her jumper was almost as big as her. Julia hurried through the beads to wash her hands and grab her apron, and Jessie snatched something off the kitchen island and held it up.

"When were you going to tell me you were replacing me?" Jessie asked, holding up the 'WE'RE HIRING' sign. "If this is about that fly in Evelyn's tea, I still stand by the fact she really should have *sensed* it was in the cup."

"She's pressing charges. The police will be here any minute. You might want to make a run for it."

"Let them come. Maybe I'll get a cell next to Molly. We can send each notes and copy each other's handwriting. Seriously, is this for real? We're hiring?"

"We're hiring," Julia said with a definite nod. "It's about time we had an extra pair of hands around here, don't you think?"

"Since about my second day, to be honest."

"Better late than never. You'll need more time off to get through your college course, and it would be nice to not juggle the schedule around the next wedding cake and murder case."

"And here I thought we were going to clone you."

"You can do the honours." Julia handed Jessie a roll of tape. "We're about to get ourselves a new co-worker."

"Who do you think it will be?"

"I have no idea," Julia said, following through the beads to take her place behind the counter as Jessie taped the sign in the door window, "and isn't that exciting?"

Thank you for reading, and don't forget to
RATE/REVIEW!

Marshmallows and Memories

The Peridale Cafe story continues in...

CARROT CAKE AND CONCERN
Coming February 28th 2023!

You can pre-order the eBook on Amazon now!

Thank you for reading!

DON'T FORGET TO RATE AND REVIEW ON AMAZON

Reviews are more important than ever, so show your support for the series by rating and reviewing the book on Amazon! Reviews are **CRUCIAL** for the longevity of any series, and they're the best way to let authors know you want more! They help us reach more people! I appreciate any feedback, no matter how long or short. It's a great way of letting other cozy mystery fans know what you thought about the book.

Being an independent author means this is my livelihood, and *every review* really does make a **huge difference.** Reviews are the best way to support me so I can continue doing what I love, which is bringing you, the readers, more fun cozy adventures!

WANT TO BE KEPT UP TO DATE WITH AGATHA FROST RELEASES? *SIGN UP THE FREE NEWSLETTER!*

www.AgathaFrost.com

You can also follow **Agatha Frost** across social media. Search 'Agatha Frost' on:

Facebook
Twitter
Goodreads
Instagram

ALSO BY AGATHA FROST

Other

Printed in Great Britain
by Amazon